Bella

A Scandalous Suffragette Novel

by Sylvia McDaniel

Books by Sylvia McDaniel

Contemporary Romance

Standalones
The Reluctant Santa
My Sister's Boyfriend
The Wanted Bride
The Relationship Coach
Her Christmas Lie
Secrets, Lies, and Online Dating
Paying for the Past
Cupid's Revenge

Anthologies
Kisses, Laughter & Love
Christmas with you

Collaborative Series

Magic, New Mexico
Touch of Decadence

Western Historicals

Standalones
A Hero's Heart
A Scarlet Bride
Second Chance Cowboy

The Cuvier Women
Wronged
Betrayed
Beguiled

Lipstick and Lead
Desperate
Deadly
Dangerous
Daring
Determined
Deceived

Scandalous Suffragettes
Abigail
Bella
Callie
Faith

The Burnett Brides
The Rancher Takes a Bride
The Outlaw Takes a Bride
The Marshal Takes a Bride
The Christmas Bride

Anthologies
Wild Western Women
Courting the West
Wild Western Women Ride Again

Collaborative Series

The Surprise Brides
Ethan

American Mail Order Brides
Katie

Bella
Published by Virtual Bookseller

Cover Design by Kim Killion
http://thekilliongroupinc.com/

Edited by Tina Winograd
www.tinaeditservices.com

Formatted by Laurelle Procter
laurelleprocter@gmail.com

Short Description: Luca Ruffini needs to sell his family's bakery
to the buyer he has lined up in order to pursue his dreams, but
the deal has been put on hold for a woman who is temptation
itself. When love blooms amidst conflicting ambitions, who will
concede?

ISBN: 978-1-942608-43-1 (paperback)
ISBN: 978-1-942608-42-4 (e-book)

{Historical Western Romance – Fiction}

www.SylviaMcDaniel.com

Synopsis

Love vs ambition!

Bella Francis is an heiress whose duty is to marry a wealthy young man of her father's choosing – which is why she ran from that life. Bella follows her friend and fellow suffragette to a western town in Texas, where she pursues owning her own bakery. She finds the perfect space, but the man who owns the building not only refuses to lease to her, but also had the nerve to spark her interest!

Luca Ruffini has a buyer for the family bakery and is in the process of selling the building to pursue his own dreams. His father, who doesn't want to sell the building, insists Luca put his plans on hold for six weeks to give Bella a chance to fulfill her passion for baking. Yet Bella is a temptation he finds himself unable to deny.

In the end, whose dream will be fulfilled and who will give up their dream for love? Who will concede?

Table of Contents

Chapter One

Nervous as a girl at her first cotillion, Bella Francis, heiress to the Francis Shipping Company out St Louis, stood in front of the podium with her best friend Abigail Vanderhooten. The Texas sun beat down on the women and the rest of the townspeople gathered to learn who had won the baking contest at the New Hope, Texas Annual Fall Festival.

The season was autumn, but the weather felt more like summer with the wind gently blowing her long skirts and teasing wisps of hair from beneath her bonnet.

She knew she was a good baker. Since the age of six, she'd spent time with Viola, her father's cook. Whenever nanny told her to occupy herself, she'd spent hours learning how to create delicious pastries, in her father's fancy kitchen. But most of all, Bella discovered she enjoyed baking.

Mayor Jack Turner walked to the front of the podium and Abigail squeezed Bella's hand. Abigail and Jack were engaged to be married as soon as the rest of their friends, their fellow suffragettes, arrived in New Hope. And that should be any day.

"That's my man," Abigail said softly gazing up at Jack with pride.

"It's okay if I don't win," Bella replied, knowing even as she said the words, she wanted this more than the college diploma she'd run from. This was her dream, her desire to own a bakery and share her love of cooking with others. And if she won this small event, then the town would realize she could bake.

"I'm pleased to announce that after ten years, we have a new champion." Jack looked down at Bella. Her heart leaped into her throat pounding furiously. "Bella Sullivan."

For a moment, she was surprised he'd said Sullivan, but she and Abigail agreed it was best she went by her grandmother's maiden name to keep her family from finding her. She knew her father was searching and didn't want to be located.

The townspeople clapped as she made her way to the podium. There, Jack handed her a blue ribbon. "You've broken the longest winning streak by Franco Ruffini. He's been our winner for the last ten festivals. Congratulations."

"Thank you," Bella said. She turned to face the judges and shook hands with the five people from the small town who had bestowed her the prize. "Thank you."

"Delicious," Mrs. Fitzgerald said. "I can't remember tasting any pastry quite so good."

The older man shook his head. "I was shocked. I didn't expect it to just melt in my mouth."

"Bella, you should open your own shop," Henrietta Mason, the owner of the restaurant told her. "The town's bakery closed when Franco took ill. You could earn a good living."

Smiling, Bella knew that was exactly what she hoped to do and was even looking at the building where the man's brick oven was located. It was the perfect set-up and she'd been considering the building since she'd arrived in New Hope. For now, her pastry goods were for sale in Abigail's mercantile. But it would be so much better if she had her own place with the right equipment.

"Thank you, Henrietta. I'll take that under advisement and consider your suggestion." She smiled at them. "Again, thank you, this means so much to me." How could she tell them it was the first good thing to happen to her in a long time, and she needed this validation that she was good at what she enjoyed doing.

Walking down the stairs, she noticed the crowd was beginning to disperse, heading over to other displays at the small festival. Actually, it was more like a town picnic compared to the events she'd attended in Boston or even in St. Louis, where she'd lived as a young girl.

Walking toward Abigail, an older, graying gentleman stepped in front of her.

"How did you convince the judges to vote for you?" he asked, his voice low and rigid.

Shocked, she shook her head. "What are you saying? I didn't say anything to the judges. They didn't know whose dish was whose."

His dark eyes flashed and he tilted his head toward them. "You talk to them."

"I was telling them thank you."

A young, dark-haired man walked up beside the older man. He glanced at her apologetically. "Papa, let it go. It was time for someone else to win."

It was then that everything fell into place.

The older man's eyes darkened as he gazed at her suspiciously. "I'm Franco Ruffini and this is my son, Luca. I'm the person whose winning streak you broke."

"I'm sorry, Mr. Ruffini."

The man's eyes narrowed and he stared at her. "I'm having a hard time believing that a young woman like yourself could out bake me."

"Papa," Luca said, gazing at her, shaking his head apologetically. "Things change."

The young man's dark hair and even darker eyes sent a tingle of awareness spiraling down her spine. He was certainly a handsome man. Even more attractive than the cowboys who roamed the town.

"My baking has not changed. It's still just as good as it used to be."

"I'm sure it is, Mr. Ruffini," Bella said, knowing the man was offended that a woman had beaten him. A young woman, an outsider in the small town.

"Next year, I will take my title back," he said, lifting his chin proudly.

She smiled. "I'm up for that challenge. Maybe before then, we can have our own bake off."

She tossed the idea out there just to appease the older gentleman.

The man tilted his head, his dark eyes suddenly brightening. A smile curved his lips and he nodded. "I accept. We'll set the time and the place."

"Papa," his son exclaimed. "Leave it alone."

The father held up his hand to silence his son. Then he reached out and took Bella's hand. "Nice to meet you, Miss Sullivan. And yes, we will set a time and a place for our bake off."

"Let me know," she said and walked away.

She tried not to laugh, but she couldn't help herself. The older man was having difficulty accepting he lost. And giving him another chance at winning seemed the nicest way to make him feel better. But she had gotten what she needed from the contest.

Now the town knew she could cook. Hopefully Abigail would help her and the two of them could find a way to get her bakery up and running.

~

The next morning, Bella was laying out her latest pastries in the mercantile when the bell above the door rang. Franco Ruffini walked through the entrance.

"Good morning," she called.

"Good morning, Miss Bella," he said. "I love your name by the way, so I hope you don't mind if I call you by your given name."

She shrugged. "That's fine. How can I help you?"

She couldn't help but wonder if his son was not far behind him. She wouldn't mind catching a glimpse of the younger Mr. Ruffini again. But she also enjoyed talking to the older gentleman. They shared a common love of baking, and she loved to hear the Italian accent that tinged his voice.

"I came to try some of your pastries. I want to taste what beat my Castagnole," he said.

Bella smiled. "I know this must be hard on you after winning for ten years."

"I'm an old man. You could have waited until I was gone before you showed me up."

A little tinge of guilt zinged its way up her spine, but then again, she'd won fairly, and it wasn't her fault the judges thought her peach turnovers the best they'd ever eaten. "I'm honored my recipe beat someone who has been the best in town for so long. It makes me feel proud."

The old man raised his brows at her. "Humph. That's nice. Now, give me one of those peach pastries and let me try it."

The old coot was certainly demanding. But she didn't think Abigail would mind that she'd let him have one of the pastries she was selling. "Here this one just came out of the oven fewer than fifteen minutes ago."

After placing the pastry on a cloth napkin she handed it to him.

Frowning at the fluffy, flaky delicacy, he took a bite and let the tastes flood his tongue. Licking his lips, his eyes darkening, he took a second bite. "Butter and a light sprinkling of sugar are on top of the baked dough."

She was impressed that he recognized the ingredients in the pastry. Some were obvious, but to admit he could taste her special touches fascinated her.

"Yes, I brushed melted butter on the dough before baking and a dash of sugar on top, which bakes into the soft flour mixture while it's in the oven."

Why was she sharing her secrets with him, when he was the one vowing to win back the title of best baker in town?

He glanced around at the store. "Why are you here? Why do you not have a bakery?"

How could she answer that question when she was hiding? She would love to own her own bakery, but she couldn't own anything until she came out of hiding. And she wasn't ready to do that just yet.

"Does this mean you like it?"

"I'm the champion you unseated. You expect me to say I think you are a better baker?" His eyes widened and grew more intense like he was angry. "Never will I admit such a thing."

Sighing, she shook her head. The old man was certainly certain of his baking abilities. "I was only inquiring if you liked the turnover. Not whether I am a better cook."

"Oh," he said sullenly. He licked his lips. "I'm still a better baker than you. But this is surprisingly good."

She almost laughed out loud. He liked her pastry, but he wasn't ready to concede defeat. She wondered what her baking teacher, Viola, would have thought of Mr. Ruffini.

"Thank you."

"What kind of oven are you using to bake these in?"

"I do what I can with what I have. I'm using my friend Abigail's stove. It's not bad." She didn't want to upset her friend by telling her the stove she was using was one of the original models. Her kitchen needed upgrading, but right now, Abigail was focused on enhancing her store.
"Besides, I do this because I enjoy working with the flour. It makes me happy."

The old man threw his hands into the air, fingers spread wide, face contorted into an expression that displayed disgust. "You cooked like this without the proper oven?"

"Yes," she said softly watching as he became almost enraged.

Suddenly, he was speaking a different language, fast, his arms flailing. She'd realized from the moment she met him that he was Italian, but it was almost comical watching him so agitated at the idea she'd used an old oven and cursing at her in his native language.

"I don't understand you."

Finally, he stopped, took a deep breath, and sighed. "Forgive me. But you have a natural God-given gift and you're not using it to your advantage."

What could she say? She was hiding from her family, hoping her father would never think to check a small town not far from Mineral Wells, Texas, where her best friend in college and her fellow suffragette lived. "It's the best I can do."

He glanced around the store. "You should have your own shop. A place where your pastries were sold. And bread."

Why she didn't was simple. No money. She'd just arrived, and until about a month ago, there was an ordinance in town that women couldn't own a business. "Maybe someday. New Hope is not exactly open to women striking out on their own and I haven't been in town long."

Though she knew in her heart, the thought of owning her own bakery had appealed for many years. But her father had not approved. He'd called it her hobby. Something to keep her occupied until she had children and social obligations like her mother. Like all women of class were expected to act. And being in the kitchen baking, was not on the list of approved skills. That was for servants.

"Long enough to beat me."

She smiled.

The bell tinkled over the door and Bella looked up to see Luca walk in. She noticed the way his long legs walked determined toward his father, his jet-black hair long in the front, but clipped closely to his ears. Seeing his father, his eyes flashed with annoyance.

"Papa, what are you doing here? She won the competition. Now, let it go," he said, coming up behind him. "I'm so sorry."

Bella smiled at the handsome man. "It's all right." She held out her hand. The man's dark eyes seemed to envelop her and warmth flooded her mid-section. "I'm Bella Sullivan."

"Luca," he said. "We sort of introduced ourselves yesterday, but I didn't want to draw any more attention than we already were."

"It's okay."

Franco gazed between the two.

"I hope he hasn't been rude."

"I am not rude," Franco said, not even looking at his son.

She laughed. Mr. Ruffini had actually made her morning quite interesting and the son was brightening her day even more. "No, we've been talking about baking. He wanted to taste my turnovers. Now, I would like to taste his Castagnole."

The old man smiled and clapped his hands. "And you shall. I will make a special batch just for you. You will taste the richness of flavor in the dough."

"I can hardly wait," Bella said, knowing she would enjoy his creation.

"Bakers have been in my family for generations," he said. "You will see."

Odd that his son hadn't taken over the bakery. She wondered what Luca did for a living.

"Do you bake?"

He shrugged. "I can, but I'd rather not."

Odd that the son seemed to almost distance himself from the very idea of working with dough.

"Papa, we need to go and let Miss Sullivan do her job."

Bella was enjoying looking at the handsome young man and his very interesting father. "Oh, it's okay. I help out Abigail and she gives me room and board. I want to earn my own living off my pastries."

Luca nodded, gaze seeming to fixate on her and she could feel herself blushing. She glanced away but spoke to the young man. "What about you, Mr. Ruffini? What do you do for a living?"

"Right now, I work in the fields."

Franco rolled his eyes and said something in Italian. She couldn't help but smile at Luca, trying to ignore his father.

"Papa, stop."

"Why should I stop? The wine is good, but the flour and the yeast go better with the wine. You need a good fresh bread to go with the wine."

Luca's face tightened with annoyance. "We really must go. My errands are done, and I must get back to work."

She looked at Franco. "I'm glad you came in this morning. I enjoy talking about baking."

The old man's eyes lit up excitedly. "Thank you, and I will bring you some Castagnole soon."

"I'm looking forward to it."

She watched them walk out and admired the way the son seemed to look out for his father. And his looks were enough to make any girl's heart beat a little faster.

~

Stepping out of the mercantile, Luca glanced at his father wishing he could rail at him about going into the store, but what could he say. He respected and loved the man, but sometimes he could cause more trouble. "Papa, why did you go see her? She won honestly."

Wagons rolled down the main street of town, dust rising from their wheels, as they walked the wooden sidewalk toward the feed store.

"Humph. I am still the best baker in this town. She has the gift, but no one bakes better pastries than Franco Ruffini," he said raising his hand in a triumphant gesture. "I don't care what the judges say."

"Well, yesterday they thought she was better," Luca reminded his father.

"They were blinded by her beauty." His father glanced up at him. "She is nice. But you're not infatuated with her, are you?"

Luca glanced at his father like he was crazy. Yes, the woman was beautiful with her dark hair curling over her shoulder, her gentle smile, and earthy brown eyes that sparkled with laughter. She'd seemed sweet and innocent and her full lips were ripe for kissing.

But he had a vineyard to plant and soil to prepare and a wine cellar to build. And women often told you what they wanted you to hear, whether they meant it or not. He didn't have time for games or love or even courting. He had his family business to make certain remained profitable.

"Of course not. My focus is not on women, but getting the vineyard up and running."

It wasn't a lie. Sure, he'd had women, but since his father's illness, life seemed more urgent. Time was running out, and he needed to replace their income.

"Good. She is not an Italian girl. Your mother and I's marriage was arranged by our parents. You should let me find you a nice Italian girl. I could contact my brother and see if he knows of anyone. Someone like your mother."

Oh dear God, that was not going to happen. "Arrange a marriage for Cara. She's almost of age."

His father shook his head vehemently. "No. I'm not ready for her to get married. Besides, you're almost twenty eight years of age. It's time."

Since his father's illness, he'd become insistent it was time for Luca to marry. This started not long after pneumonia almost killed Franco. The doctor had not expected him to live, but at sixty years of age, he was once again healthy and now that they'd made the decision to close the bakery, Luca thought he was often bored.

"When it's right, I'll meet a girl. But until then, I've got work to do."

Yes, Luca was working very hard right now. But he didn't want to take a chance on his father ruining his health again. He didn't want him getting up early and going to the bakery. He didn't want him standing on his feet all day, either baking or dealing with customers. This was Franco's time to rest and enjoy life. While Luca learned the family business and expanded it in a new direction as he took care of his brother and sister.

"And if you only work and never enjoy the arms of a woman or the pleasure of their company, you will be a very dull man. Your mother, God rest her soul, gave me the happiest years of my life. She showed me what was important. You think you know what is important in life, but you're all work and no play."

If Luca didn't love his family so much, he would have left. But they were everything, even when his father was being difficult. "Papa, once the vineyard is up and running, then I will either find some girl to marry or I will let you find me a woman."

Franco shook his head, raising his hand dramatically. "The vineyard will not be fully functional for several years. The vines, they take time to mature and grow. I told you we should never have closed the bakery."

"And I told you I didn't want to walk in one day and find you dead on the floor."

His father shrugged nonchalantly like it didn't matter, but it did to Luca. He'd already lost one parent; he wasn't ready to lose his father.

"I would have died a happy man amongst the flour."

"The doctor said for you not to be on your feet working twelve to fourteen hours a day."

"But I enjoyed what I was doing."

They had this same argument at least once a week and Luca knew his response by heart.

"Then do it at home."

"It's not the same."

"If you want to see me married and with bambinos then you can't be working in the bakery. Plus Cara and Ricci, they want their father to be around when they're grown."

His father sighed. "One day you will face this challenge from your son. And you won't like it."

"And I will remember our conversation. But until then, you should enjoy your life."

Franco was silent as they walked through the small town to the wagon sitting out front of the feed store. "You could be in your thirties before the vineyard is producing wine."

"You're repeating yourself. Drop it, Papa," Luca said.

Right now, he didn't have time for a woman. So much was hanging on him selling the bakery. Then he could purchase the wine making equipment he needed. The bottles, corks, and barrels. There was so much to do, and yet, Bella Sullivan was someone who he couldn't help but think about.

The woman intrigued him. She'd beaten his father at the festival and no one had ever out baked his father. And then today, she'd accepted the old man coming over to challenge her win. It was like they seemed to understand one another and that surprised him.

Yes, Bella Sullivan was an interesting woman, but he didn't have time to explore her soft curves or the fullness of her delicious mouth.

Chapter Two

At dinner that night, after the mercantile had closed at five, Jack Turner, Abigail's fiancé sat at the head of the table. Once her friends arrived, they would be wed. Bella couldn't help but think how far they all had come since the day they'd spent in jail almost three months ago. They'd marched upon a bank in Boston that refused to give women loans and found themselves locked up.

After that, Abigail returned home to New Hope to take care of her ailing father. A week after Abigail left, Bella received a telegram stating her father would be arriving in Boston to take her back to St Louis. He'd found a man to marry her. She had packed her bags and boarded the next train to Fort Worth and then taken a stage to New Hope.

Abigail had invited their friends to help her change the town, and Bella couldn't wait for them to arrive and see the task before them.

"When do you think the suffragettes will arrive?" Bella asked.

"Any day," Abigail said, smiling at Jack who shook his head. "I'm sure they had to wrap up things in Boston before they headed west. And not everyone will come, but still, it will be great to see who decides to try their luck here and who stays in Boston."

"Do you think Diamond will come?" Bella asked, thinking of their flamboyant friend whose family life was the stuff dime novels were made of.

"Yes, I think Diamond and Callie will come. Emma's in medical school, and last I heard, Faith went back to college. Georgia may come, but I don't know for certain, and Haley went home to get married. So at least three might show up on our doorstep. I can't wait."

It would be so good to see their friends again. And to watch the reaction of this small town to the women's attempts to modernize the west.

Jack groaned. "You ladies are going to be the death of me. First, my lovely Abigail annihilates a law that has been on the books for years, and now three more of you strong-willed women will arrive and try to stay out of trouble and keep the men in this town happy. This is my last year of being mayor. Someone else can take on this task."

Abigail smiled at Jack and reached over and patted him on the hand. "That's because you're going to be very busy opening your new apothecary next door."

"We should start taking a serious look at property for the suffragettes to rent for their businesses," Bella said, knowing she was thinking of herself. She wished she could dip into her trust fund and build herself a bakery, but she knew that was impossible. Touching her trust fund would be a road map to her whereabouts. Wouldn't Daddy love that?

Somehow she was going to find a way to build her bakery, even if that meant she did nothing but sell her items in Abigail's mercantile until she had the cash she needed. She would go to the bank, but they might alert her father to her desire for her funds. And that wouldn't do, at all. The one thing she wanted as much as her own bakery was staying hidden from her father and his choice of her bridegroom.

"Whoa, wait just a minute," Jack said. "Let's not put the cart before the horse. We don't know for certain that the women are going to arrive."

"Oh, they'll be here," Abigail said with certainty. "Think of it this way, once they arrive we'll be able to set a date for our wedding."

The man grinned. "Then I guess all the trouble coming with their arrival will be okay."

Abigail had stayed the biggest hurdle for the women. She'd gotten the city to cancel and rewrite the law regarding women owning a business. Now everyone could open a store or a place to sell their goods and wares.

Bella laughed, she couldn't help herself. "In a town that doesn't want women to own property, a business, or do anything besides take care of their families, what makes you think five single suffragette women can make a difference."

Abigail snickered.

"Because if they're like you and Abigail, this town has no idea the trouble headed their way."

The women glanced at each other and smiled. Bella knew this town needed shaking up. Sure, women had limitations placed on them, but in this town, they expected you to almost walk behind your husband instead of beside him. And there was no way any man was going to get her to follow him like a blind person.

"All we want is to be able to make a choice on whether or not we want to marry. Not that we have to marry in order to own or run a business, a bank account, or even get a loan. We just want to live our lives in a way that shows we are strong women who like and want a man for something other than his paycheck and ability to take care of us," Bella said softly, her voice full of strength.

Women had so few rights. It wasn't only the fact they couldn't vote. If a woman decided to leave her husband, she gave up everything. Her home, her children, her money, and anything else the couple had obtained while married. If your man died, it was difficult for you to move or have access to the family money. The bankers wanted to deal with men, not women.

"Oh, Lord," Jack said. "Right there is why this town is in so much trouble. Abigail has gotten one law changed, and yesterday you beat a man who has reigned as top baker in this town for as long as I can remember. Yet, your peach turnover beat his Castagnole. Change is happening faster than I think the men here are prepared for, and now you've got recruits arriving to help you. New Hope is in for a bumpy ride."

But once they became accustomed to women running businesses and doing something besides catering to their husbands, this would be a sweet place to live. Or at least, she hoped so.

Abigail lifted her wine glass and clinked it against Bella's and Jack's. "To new beginnings and strong, independent women."

They set their wine glasses down and Bella glanced at Jack while she cut a piece of meat. "Tell me about Franco Ruffini. He came by the mercantile this morning to ask about my baking until his son took him away."

She really wanted to ask more about Luca, but hoped when he told her about Franco, he would also mention the son.

Jack shrugged. "They're a nice Italian family who moved here twenty years ago, at least. Franco and his wife ran the bakery until the mother died. Then Franco and his son tried to continue the bakery until Franco came down with pneumonia and almost died. I think the bakery holds lots of memories for them."

Turning toward Jack, Abigail frowned. "What happened to the building the bakery occupied?"

"Oh, it's down the street, up for sale," Jack said.

Bella felt a tingle travel the length of her spine. It was a silent message of excitement and thrill. Maybe she could somehow purchase the building from the family.

"Bella, you should think about buying that building," Abigail said, her voice rising in excitement.

If only she could get to her trust fund, the building would most certainly be hers. But maybe there was some other way.

"And how would you suggest I purchase it?" Bella asked. "I can't afford it without getting my father involved, and well, I'm not ready to deal with that drama."

Jack frowned as he took a bite of steak.

"No, but you could rent it from Luca. If it's just sitting empty, and if it has great ovens, just think of the pastries, cakes, and breads you could create. And since they closed, there is no bakery in town."

Leasing the building was not a bad idea. He would be receiving money and she would have a building to do her cooking.

"People love fresh bread," Jack replied. "Luca comes into town on Mondays and takes his sister to piano lessons at Mrs. Jackson's house. Usually he sits outside in the wagon or comes by the saloon and waits. You might catch him alone then and see if he would be interested in leasing the space."

A shiver rippled through her at the thought of going into the saloon to meet with him. But she would if she had to. She only hoped she'd catch him outside the Jackson house so they could talk alone.

Would he rent the space to her, and could she make enough money to keep a business going?

~

On Monday, Bella walked through town in the direction of Mrs. Jackson's house, her gloved hands shaking, a parasol shading her face from the blistering rays of the hot Texas sun. In St. Louis, there had been hot days, but the nights were cooler and fall was a pleasant time.

Here, the sun just continued to shine brightly, and so far, the trees had not started to drop their leaves. Her shoes

clip-clopped along the wooden sidewalk before she turned
to a residential area and walked up the dusty street toward
the house hoping that today was not the day Luca decided
to wait in the saloon.

When she turned on the street where Mrs. Jackson
lived, she saw him sitting in the buggy, his hat pulled low
over his head, his legs stretched out, waiting. She walked
up to the wagon. His body was long and lean, and she had
the strangest urge to run her hands down his muscled arms.

"Excuse me, Mr. Ruffini," she said softly, hoping he
wasn't really sleeping.

He jumped and looked down at her. "Miss Sullivan," he
said sitting up straight and putting his hat on his head.

She always was startled when people called her by that
name. She would never get used to it and couldn't wait for
the day when she could reveal her real name. But then,
maybe that day would never come. She didn't know.

"Sorry to disturb you, but could I have a moment of
your time?"

"Sure," he said and jumped down from the wagon. His
feet slapping the ground right in front of her. She leaned
her head back and peeked up at him from her bonnet.

Licking her lips nervously, she gazed into his dark eyes
and felt a rush of warmth spread through her. There was
something about this man that intrigued her. She wanted to
learn more about him, yet she knew that wasn't possible.
Not with her family searching for her.

"I peered in the window of the old bakery and
wondered do the ovens still work?"

"Of course," he said his eyes staring at her puzzled.
"Why do you want to know?"

A trickle of excitement scurried through her at the
thought of leasing this space. She wanted it so badly. It was
the answer to her prayers and perfect for what she wanted
to do.

"I know you're trying to sell the building and I'm unable to buy it from you for now, but I was wondering if it would be possible for me to lease that space from you. I want to start a bakery and your building is already setup. It would be perfect."

She watched as he stared, his eyes widening. "You know, even if I hadn't sold the building a couple of weeks ago, I still would not let you open your bakery in my family's old location. It just seems wrong to let you, the woman who somehow outdid my father, take over his bakery."

Bella stepped back a little stunned. The son was angry at her because she'd beat his father at the bake off? Ridiculous. "I'm sorry. I didn't know it would upset you that I beat his father."

"My family means everything to me and while I understand you outdid him fairly, I just couldn't let you put your business in where my family has worked so hard for so many years."

What could she say? In her own clan, she loved them, but she also did not have this need to protect them like he obviously did. His father seemed like a strong gentleman who could get by on his own.

"I see it differently. The space your father produced so many great cakes and breads in would continue to honor his work by hopefully producing the same quality of food as his. It would be an honor to bake in his ovens and share the space where he once worked."

Luca looked toward the house and then down at her. "Even if that were so, I've made a commitment to a buyer and he intends to finalize the plans in the next three weeks. The bakery is no longer available."

An ache began in the center of her chest. She'd gotten her hopes and dreams up, and now they were once again dashed. She sighed and felt her shoulders release the tension. "I understand. But please, don't think that because I beat your father at the Fall Festival that I would dishonor his baking in any way. He won for a long time."

Why were they all taking this so personally? Was it because the older man had won so long that they had never considered someone else would eventually win? Or were they all angry she had beaten the older gentleman.

"Why are you being so nice to my father?"

"Why not? We share a love of baking."

Bella held nothing but respect for this man's father and even hoped that someday they could bake together. She probably would learn a lot from the gentleman.

Just then the door opened and a young girl came bouncing down the steps, almost running to the wagon. "I'm done, Luca."

She stopped when she saw Bella. The girl looked so much like Luca, but her eyes sparkled with merriment. "Hello, I'm Cara."

Bella held out her hand. "I'm Bella Sullivan."

The girl's eyes widened. "You're the lady who beat our papa at the baking contest."

Oh, dear. If Bella had known the contest was going to give her this much grief, maybe she should never have entered. "Yes, I won."

The girl tilted her head and smiled. "Papa came home last night talking about your turnovers. He said they were really good."

"Thank you. I'm honored he thought so," Bella said, glancing at Luca.

The girl looked at her brother and then back at Bella. "You should come to dinner some night. I'm sure you and Papa would have a lot of things to talk about."

Bella glanced at Luca, unable to hide the smile on her face. The brother didn't want her near his family bakery and the sister wanted her to come to dinner. "Thank you, but I don't know if that's such a good idea."

"We need to go," Luca said, running his hand through his hair nervously. "Sorry, Miss Sullivan, but you'll need to find somewhere else to have a bakery."

"Yes, I will."

Again, she was not going to let him stop her. Now that she had decided this was what she wanted, she would do everything in her power to make it happen.

His sister's eyes widened. "You wanted to open the bakery again?"

Bella nodded her head. "I wanted to lease the building from your family. But your brother tells me it's not available."

Cara turned and glanced at her brother with the oddest expression.

"We have to go. Good evening," Luca said.

Luca helped his sister into the wagon and then crawled in beside her. He clucked to the horses and the wagon pulled away, leaving Bella standing in the street. With a sigh, she turned and headed to the mercantile. She'd have to keep looking. She wanted to open a bakery and she wouldn't let this or any man stop her. But in the meantime, there was bread rising that probably needed her attention.

~

Luca was lost in thought as they headed out to the vineyard. His mother insisted they buy the land before she died. They planned on it being where his parents spent their last years. After he shut down the bakery, they made the decision to move from town and live full-time at the vineyard. A decision they didn't regret.

"Bella seems like a nice girl."

"I guess," he said, thinking about the woman's proposal. The buyer was in hand. He couldn't walk away from the chance of selling the building outright.

Yet, he still had qualms about giving up his family's bakery. And the lovely Miss Sullivan almost scared him. All he could do was stare at her full lips and wonder how they would feel beneath his own and was her skin as silky to the touch as it looked. He so wanted to trail his fingers down her face, to touch her.

Sighing he tried to keep his focus on getting home and not on how the woman had awakened him to how much he missed a woman's touch. He'd had girlfriends, but nothing serious. Flirtations that ended almost as quickly as they started.

"Why don't you want to lease the bakery to her? It would be one way of keeping the bakery running. Everyone in town has complained about the lack of fresh bread available. We could even take a small portion of her sales."

He glanced at his sister. Where had she learned how to be so innovative in business? "I guess we could. But I'd rather just sell it out right. Then I could take that money and put it into the vineyard. Besides, the idea of someone other than our family in that kitchen...well, it bothers me."

She shook her head at him. "Beneath that tough male exterior, you are such a softy. You're like dough. Marry the girl, and then we'd still have family in the kitchen."

His sister could believe what she wanted, but Luca knew he tried to make his papa happy with how he was running the business.

Luca laughed. "And you, sister, are a dreamer. I'm not getting married anytime soon. Are you going to start in on me like Papa?"

"No, but I was just throwing out a solution. She's a baker. She's one of us."

Maybe that's what frightened him most of all about Miss Sullivan. She was attractive, and she loved to bake.

"Yes, well, she also beat our father in a contest he's won for years."

"But that just shows how good a baker she is. You know Papa is the best and for her to beat him, that makes her exceptional." She sighed. "I watched you two. There is something there you are ignoring. You like her, and well, I think she would fit into our family."

He had to shut Cara up before they reached the house or his father would be jumping all over the idea of him and Bella.

"Would you stop? Don't let Papa hear you saying these things to me or I will convince him to send you off to a nunnery."

She laughed. "No, you wouldn't. You'd miss me."

"Like rat poison."

"Ha!" she said. "You know it's okay for you to like a woman. You can still be the head of the family and have a girlfriend."

Yes, he had been a little focused on trying to make sure he didn't lose their money. After all, his father had entrusted him when he had gotten sick, and Luca wanted to do a good job.

"It's a lot more responsibility than I anticipated. I just want to make Papa proud."

"And you will. But you'd make him even happier if you found a wife."

Why was it that everyone thought if you didn't have someone by your side that you were missing out on life? When he fell in love, he wanted to have time to spend with his wife and children. He didn't want to be so focused on the vineyard and the family business that he couldn't enjoy his marriage. Now was just not the right time.

Luca groaned. "I'm going to change everyone's focus from me finding a wife to you finding a husband. You are old enough. Our mother was married when she was your age."

"And who would you choose for me?"

Luca thought for a long moment. There was no one in town he wanted near his little sister. In fact, he'd fight any man that tried. But he knew sooner or later, someone would choose her and he just hoped it was someone who treated her right, otherwise, they would answer to him.

"See, you answered my question. There is no one in New Hope that even interests me. So I'm safe. You, on the other hand. I think someone has arrived that has put a twinkle in your eyes, a smile on your face, and a spring in your step. Oh yeah, you can deny it all you want, but Bella Sullivan intrigues you."

"Stop. Now you're just creating drama."

But she wasn't and he knew it. There was something about the girl that drew him to her. Right now was just not the time for her to show up in his life. He didn't have time for a woman. Especially a woman who enjoyed baking like she did because she would fit into his family so well.

"Promise me you won't say anything to Papa about Miss Sullivan wanting to rent the bakery."

If his father found out, he would probably give it to her, just to stop him from selling the place.

"Why?"

"Because I don't want him upset. And I haven't told him I have a buyer for the place."

That was one fight he wasn't looking forward to. Sure his father had agreed to put the "For Sale" sign on the door, but he hadn't believed anyone would want the building. Now Luca had a buyer and someone who wanted to lease the space.

"Good luck convincing him to sell. I don't think he will."

"We've talked about it, but I don't know. We'll have to wait and see."

Cara shook her head at him. "I think you're going to be disappointed. He and Mama spent so many years working side by side there that I doubt he will go through with the sale. It's one thing to talk about getting rid of the place, but it's another to actually sell his business."

His sister could be right. That's why he was waiting until everything was ready and then he would tell his father. Hopefully the amount of money would be enough that he wouldn't hesitate to sell.

"I know. So I'm waiting until the buyer is all lined up. Then I'll bring it to him."

"Just lease the place to the girl."

"No," he said. "Not unless I have to."

If he leased the bakery to Bella, he would feel compelled to go by and check on it almost daily and seeing another person where his family had worked so hard, well...he didn't know if he could do it. Not even the beautiful Bella.

Chapter Three

As the morning light brightened the window, Franco stood over the pan where he was frying dough. Looking up, he watched his daughter come traipsing down the stairs. With her long, dark hair she reminded him of his wife and his heart ached with longing for Maria. She'd been gone two years, three months, and nine days. And not a day went by he didn't miss her touch.

"Good morning, Papa," his sweet angel said, coming to kiss him on the cheek.

"Good morning, love."

"Why are you frying Castagnole for breakfast?"

She reached for one sitting on the counter, waiting for him to dust with the sugar he'd ground. "These are not for you. These are for Miss Sullivan."

His daughter laughed. "That woman has managed to bewitch the men in this family. Don't let Ricci near her or you will all be under her spell."

When did Cara meet the young woman? And why did she believe Luca and him were enthralled with the girl. "What are you talking about? I want her to experience my pastry. When did you meet her?"

Cara walked away from her father and sat at the table. "We saw her in town yesterday when Luca took me to my piano lesson. She seems really nice, and I do think my brother is a little enchanted by her."

A smile spread across Franco's face. He'd thought the same thing when he'd witnessed Bella and Luca talking. From what he could see, she would be a great match for his son. She loved to bake and maybe she could convince Luca to open the bakery. Oh, to be working amongst the flour and yeast again.

"What makes you think your brother likes this girl?"

"The way his eyes sparkle when he talks to her and how he can't seem to take his gaze off her. He just seems to watch her and forget that anyone else is around. It kind of reminded me of the way you and Mama used to act."

"God rest her soul," Franco said, his heart banging with longing for his lost wife. She would know exactly what to do in this situation with their son. She could say the perfect thing that would make his boy wake up and realize there was an opportunity right in front of him.

But when Franco tried to connect with Luca and convince him to do something, he went in the opposite direction. Over and over again, his son did this until Franco did his best not to say anything.

"You know your brother. If we suggested she would be a girl he should consider, he would run so fast in the opposite direction..."

"That we'd never see him again," Cara finished for her father. "I think we should try something different. You know, tell him to leave her alone. That he should avoid her and see his reaction."

Franco thought about what his daughter was proposing. It wasn't a bad suggestion. He lifted the last of the Castagnole from the pan. In Italy, these were served at carnival time, but here in Texas, he served them whenever there was a special occasion. Gently blotting the extra oil from the tender fried dough, he left them cooling and turned back to his daughter.

"What did you think of the girl?"

His daughter grinned. "I immediately liked her. Of course, I still believe my father is the best baker in town, but she would fit in the family. She's one of us."

That's what he'd been thinking and to hear Cara thought that Luca was attracted to the girl, pleased him immensely.

Nodding he hugged his daughter to him. "La mia bellissima figlia, you are not only beautiful but very smart.

I think you are right about Miss Sullivan and your brother. If we try to push the two of them together, he will bolt. So let's encourage him that she is not for him."

Cara laughed. "Oh, Papa, if I am smart, I learned everything from you."

He beamed. His wife had given him three beautiful children who he loved with all his heart. But it was time for them to start spreading their wings and finding their own way in life. Especially, Luca. It was passed time. And he hated that the bakery was sitting empty, the ovens not in use. What if Bella would like to fire up the bakery again? Was she the person to convince his son the bakery was still important?

~

The bell dinged above the door of the mercantile just as Bella came out of the kitchen carrying the day's baking into the store.

"Mr. Ruffini, it's so good to see you," she said. "What did you bring?"

The man was carrying a basket lined with dish towels that covered something. She knew he must be bringing her a sample of his entry at the Fall Festival.

"I brought you Castagnole."

The smell of fresh, baked yeast accosted her senses. She hoped the pastry tasted as good as its smell promised and that Mr. Ruffini was an excellent baker. She would hate if she couldn't be honest and tell him the pastry was delicious.

She glanced at Abigail stocking shelves. She waved him to the back. "There's fresh coffee in the kitchen. Please, join me and we'll enjoy coffee and your Castagnole."

"Thank you," he said, carefully following her to the kitchen.

Quickly, she poured two cups of coffee and sat at the table. "I can hardly wait to try these."

Putting the pastry to her mouth, her teeth sank into the crispy dough on the outside and the bread like center. There was just a hint of something she didn't recognize. "Hmmm...this is delicious. But what is that flavor I can't distinguish? I'm sure there're eggs and sugar, but what else?"

"Rum," he said. "One tablespoon of rum gives it that unique flavor."

Liquor? That surprised her and yet the taste was wonderful and she knew the alcohol had cooked into the dough.

"It's delicious. No wonder you've won all these years. It just melts in your mouth. I need another," she said picking up one from the basket.

He laughed. "I'm glad you're enjoying them."

She ate another and knew the pastry was delicious, and that she'd been lucky to win against this obvious master of baking.

"Over a year ago, I took ill and they didn't think I was going to live."

"I'm so sorry to hear that and glad to see you've proven them wrong," she said, thinking about her own father. How would she feel if he became ill or suddenly passed away? Life was too precious and often slipped away too quickly. And yet they were estranged and miles from one another.

"At the time, it was all Luca could do to run the bakery and also try to take care of me and Cara and Ricci, my other children. My wife's been dead for over two years, and frankly, I think I almost died from missing her."

Bella's heart wrenched at the man's admission. It was so obvious he loved his family and she wished her own father was more like Franco.

"You're going to make me cry," she said.

He patted her hand. "My prayer is that all of my children someday find the kind of love I had with their mother. But what I wanted to tell you, is my family still owns the bakery. It's been sitting empty since I took ill. Would you be interested in opening it back up?"

The old man's face seemed eager as if he were sharing his love for the place with her. "Of course, I would love to come and help you and even teach you some things. But you're a good baker and I'm an old man who just likes to play in the flour occasionally.

"I don't want to work the counter or be there every day. But a couple of times a week, it would do me good to get out of the house and back to what I enjoyed."

Had Luca not told him he'd sold the bakery? She was not going to be the one who broke this precious man's heart by telling him his son had already sold the building. No, that would be his son's job. But she had offered to lease the space and Luca obviously hadn't told him she'd approached him with this same idea.

Dropping her eyes, she sighed. Her chest wrenched with pain, her throat tight with unshed tears. She'd so badly wanted that bakery and she didn't want to upset Franco, but she wasn't going to lie to him either. Her decision made, she glanced up and stared into the same shade of dark eyes that Luca had.

"You show me great honor by offering to let me work in your family bakery. But I spoke to Luca yesterday about this same idea and he told me it was impossible. You see, I thought your ovens are sitting there not being used and I wanted to lease the space from him. But he told me that wasn't possible."

"Why?" Franco said, throwing his hands up in the air. "Why would my son not accept your offer?"

"He told me the bakery was his family's and he would not let the woman who had outdone his father take over the building."

Franco laughed. "He's been trying to sell the family bakery, so I don't understand his loyalty all of a sudden."

She shrugged. She knew, but she wasn't going to say another word to Franco. This was between him and his son. "I told him I would be honored to bake in the same ovens, but he said no."

Franco stood, his eyes darkening and she knew he was angry, but what could she do. She'd been honest with him, but she hadn't told him everything. And once he learned his son had sold the business, then she feared he would be consumed with rage.

"This matter is not closed. I will speak with my son and get back with you. You would be responsible for the business."

"I offered to pay him rent," she said softly.

He spoke rapid fire Italian and she felt certain there were curse words but was not going to ask.

"Bella, I will speak with my son. Don't be searching for any other location just yet. Let me talk with him and then one of us will get back with you."

"I don't want to cause problems between you," she said.

Shaking his head, his hands clenched at his side, he gazed at her. "We are two stubborn Italian males. Of course, there is going to be problems between us, but there is also love of family. That is most important. You will hear from us soon."

Part of her didn't want to get her hopes up and the other part was trying not to show too much excitement. She'd been wrong to go to Luca and should have started with Franco to achieve her dream. He wanted to reopen the bakery as well and would also give her advice.

She reached into the basket and pulled out one more Castagnole. The pastries were delicious.

"Keep them," he said smiling at her. "Are you sure you are not Italiano?"

She shrugged. "I don't know. I think we're French, but I'm not even certain about that. I'll return the basket to you."

She walked him to the door of the mercantile. "Good day, Mr. Ruffini. And thank you for bringing me your pastries. They were delicious."

He smiled. "Good day."

After he left the store, she hurried over to Abigail rearranging shelves, barely able to contain herself. Maybe everything was going to come together and she'd finalize the deal on the bakery after all. But whatever happened, she felt like beating Mr. Ruffini had been a life changing event. Now she hoped it was for the good.

"He's going to talk to his son about letting me have the bakery." She jumped up and down so excited. "But I fear his son is going to be so angry with me."

~

Luca had risen early this morning and left the house before his father and siblings were even up. He'd been busy all day in the fields prepping the soil for the vines he would soon plant. Plus he'd been tying up the overloaded vines, getting them ready for harvest. They were just weeks away from the largest crop of grapes he'd grown. At lunchtime, he went into the barn to clean up before he went into the house.

His father entered the barn and walked toward him. "Hi, Papa."

"Why did you not want to lease the bakery to Miss Sullivan," he said his voice rising.

A twinge of nerves zinged up Luca's spine at the angry tone of his father. How had he found out about Luca turning the woman down? "It's your bakery, Papa. It's the family's bakery and I couldn't let a stranger work in yours and Mama's kitchen."

The old man crossed his arms over his chest. "But you want to sell this sacred family building. Is that not the same thing?"

Already Luca could feel his defenses building. That baking contest had stirred up not only his father but brought Bella Sullivan into their lives. Another week and the sale would have been behind him and none of this would have mattered.

One of the horses in the stalls neighed nervously at the sound of his father's voice. Luca wiped his hands on a rag and faced his father.

"The person I hope to sell to is not going to run a bakery out of the building."

Maybe he was crazy, and it wasn't like he wanted to run the place. He'd never enjoyed working with the flour like his mama and papa. They'd wanted him to learn and he had begrudgingly, but it just wasn't what he enjoyed doing. He loved working in the fields, babying the grapes until the sugar was high and just right to make wine.

"So my ovens will do what? Will they be destroyed? Life happens, things change and I would rather my ovens were being used than sitting idle," he said, his voice rising even higher as he raised his hands in the air. "Maybe your brother or your sister will take up the art of creating pastries."

Luca had to lick his lips. "I have a buyer for the place. We hope to close next week."

The smell of manure assaulted his nose and he wanted to tell the horse thanks for making this situation even more undesirable.

"And do what with the building?" Franco asked.

"He plans on tearing it down and build a hotel."

His father cursed in Italian, which Luca understood. He'd known he would not be elated with his decision to sell the place, but the building was sitting empty. A shrine to what was once a happy place. A place filled with love and joy between his parents. He had great memories of them all working there together. But it was over. His mother was dead and his father had almost died from trying to run the bakery by himself.

There was silence for a moment. "And you think this is better than someone working where your mother and I spent the best times of our lives together?"

What could he say? Neither option was good. "No, but you know I need the money from the sale to put into the vineyard."

"That damn vineyard has not earned us a dime, but the bakery could be bringing in cash every day."

"And you would be right back there working in it every day."

His father stopped and frowned and Luca knew he was right. Since he'd lost at the Fall Festival, it was like he wanted to regain his title and he needed the connection of the bakery to do that. But Luca feared that would kill him and he wasn't ready for his papa to die.

"If I sell the bakery, you will not be rising before dawn to prepare the bread and staying late at night to work the books. The business consumed you until the point you fell ill."

"And your vineyard does not consume you?"

What could he say? Just because he was out with the vines nearly seven days a week, checking and watching and waiting for the fruit to turn ripe.

"Yes, it does. But I'm not sixty years old."

"Not yet."

"I hoped that you would spend this time to enjoy the life you and Mama created. You deserve the time off."

His father's eyes flashed at him, and he clenched his fists. "You do not understand. I'm bored. I know I can no longer work the long hours I did in the past. But I at least could come in several days a week and work with the dough. I could enjoy the smell of baking bread and visit with my old customers again. You say you don't want to see anyone else use the family ovens, but I disagree. It is better that the bakery continues on as it was. Tearing it down is wrong."

Somehow he had to convince his father this was the only way. They needed the influx of cash for the vineyard. Hopefully in the next year they would produce their first bottles of wine and then the cash would start to flow again.

"Papa, I have a buyer."

His father held up his hand. "No. I'm not ready to sell. Give me six weeks to work with Miss Sullivan. If she can't make the bakery profitable and running smoothly, I will concede and let you sell the family business. But I insist on this six weeks."

Time enough for the buyer to lose interest. Time enough for winter to arrive and the material he needed to make the wine. He had more grapes than ever before, but no cellar to store the wine and no bottles to strain the liquid into after it was filtered.

"Papa," Luca said with annoyance. "That woman has no idea how to run the bakery, and I don't have time to teach her."

His father's voice rose in defiance. "I have given over the family money and business to you to handle. I'm letting you learn and hoping everything I've taught you will keep the family going. I'm giving you the opportunity. Now you should, in turn, give Miss Sullivan a chance."

Luca stared at his father wanting to yell right back at him, but knowing that would not be good. As it was, their voices had already been raised. This threw everything off, but what could he do? The bakery and the money were his father's. He had to listen to him and obey, even though his own plans would be delayed.

"I'll ask the buyer to wait six weeks. But after that if the bakery is not a success this means we sell the building."

He could only pray the buyer would be willing to wait until his papa was ready to let go of the building.

"Miss Sullivan has the flour flowing in her blood, she will be successful. Six weeks we will know for certain."

Disappointment fueled by rage coursed through Luca, springing him into action. He couldn't sit quietly and have lunch. No, it was imperative he speak with Miss Sullivan and hope she understands what she's done.

Somehow this woman had managed to hypnotize his father and now she'd ruined his arrangements. Luca had told her no and she'd gone behind his back and approached his father. Now all Luca's plans were put on hold while he had to deal with Miss Sullivan.

Walking out of the barn, his father followed him. "Where are you going?"

"Into town to talk to the buyer," he said, knowing full well he was going to warn Miss Sullivan away from his father.

"Oh, do you want me to come with you?"

"No," he said. "I can handle it."

And handle it he would. Miss Sullivan was going to wish she'd never interfered and gotten her way. If possible, Luca was going to make it extremely difficult for her to be successful.

~

Bella was happily putting another tray of cookies into the oven when she heard Abigail talking to someone. It sounded like Luca. She peeked around the corner of the kitchen and saw him standing there, his arms crossed across his chest, his eyes dark and his mouth set tightly. He certainly didn't appear too happy.

"Bella," he yelled.

Good grief, what was going on for him to be shouting her name? Wiping her hands on her dirty apron, she walked up front. "Why are you roaring like a lion?"

"I told you she was busy," Abigail said and walked away.

"You know why," he said. "You went to my father," he said angrily, his voice rising.

"I did not," she responded quietly. She walked from behind the counter and glanced around the store. She was not going to have this obvious argument in front of customers. But she didn't see anyone in the store, so they were safe for now. "Your father came to see me today and brought me Castagnole. We talked about baking and he mentioned to me, that I should use his bakery. I told him I had spoken to you and you told me that was not possible. I didn't even mention you had sold the bakery."

Luca tilted his head to the side and gazed at her. She could see he was trying to decide if he believed her or not and that just made her angrier. "Your father has been extremely kind to me. We both enjoy baking and he offered to show me some techniques. He's the one who mentioned letting me use the bakery. Not me."

Her tone was just as tense as his. This handsome man didn't deserve to have a father like Franco Ruffini who was a kind, generous man. And his attitude made her long for the money in her trust fund. She'd like nothing better than to buy the bakery from Luca and ask his father to come in and bake whenever he felt like it. He would always have an open door if she had her way.

"I don't know why he is so infatuated with you and your cooking. But he is now insisting you be given six weeks to run the bakery before he will let me sell the place."

Inside Bella was dancing and crying like a little girl, she was filled with such excitement. But Luca was angry and she feared he would be difficult the next six weeks.

"I didn't suggest he let me use the bakery, he did."

Luca shook his head, his mouth set in an angry line. "Fine, you will have full run of the bakery for six weeks only. But my papa will come and work there some, but I don't want him there more than three to four hours a day, do you understand me?"

"Of course. He's welcome there as long as he wants to work."

"I'm not going to let you overwork my father to the point it kills him. In six weeks, if you're not making a profit, then I will be selling the building. And believe me, Miss Sullivan, I don't think there is any way you will be able to make a profit. Even if your cooking is excellent. It took my father years to build that business."

Of all the arrogant, challenges to throw down, this was one. It just made her want to show him how she would make a profit.

"Why, is my baking not good enough or is it because I'm a woman?" she asked her hands on her hips.

Why were all men such presumptuous oafs that didn't think a woman could do anything besides take care of them?

"I've seen how hard my family worked to keep the bakery going, I don't think there is any way you can do it on your own. It's not that you aren't a good cook. It's because it took all of us working it full-time. It wore my father out and I think was probably why my mother died so early," he said gazing defiantly at her.

And that's where his assumptions would get him into trouble. Who said she would be doing this alone?

"But now you've got what you want. You will be in control for six weeks in order to make my papa happy. But don't ask for one day longer. Because I have a buyer and I will be selling that building, six weeks and one day later."

"And if I'm successful?"

He laughed. "You are one mere woman."

"Oh, you have no idea what you've just said. I may look like one mere, small, delicate woman, but you've just created a firestorm," she said, her voice low and urgent. Now she was angry and she would do whatever it took to beat him at his own game. "Abigail?"

"Yes," she called from the back.

"Luca Ruffini doesn't believe I can make the bakery successful by myself."

She laughed. "Who said you would be doing it alone? The suffragettes are on their way here. They'll help you."

He frowned. "Suffragettes? What is this term? I don't know it."

"We're fighting for women's rights. The right to make decisions on our own. To have a bank account. Own a business, and make that business successful. My friends are on their way, and they will help make this bakery very successful. I won't be alone, Mr. Ruffini. My friends are coming to help."

Italian words spewed from his mouth.

"Stop," she said. "I don't know what you're saying, but it's probably not very nice, so please don't use that language in front of me."

For all she knew he could have been calling her beautiful names, but she didn't care. He'd angered her to the point that now she wanted him gone so she could get started on preparing the bakery.

He threw his hands in the air. "Please. You're killing me. I can't let you have the bakery any longer than six weeks."

She smiled at him, feeling just a little bad for him. He'd just made a horrible deal for himself. "A deal is a deal. If the bakery is successful, I will continue to lease it from you until I can purchase the building from you."

His eyes widened and she could see the anger seeming to explode from within him, but he only grimaced, nodded his head in her direction. "Good day, Miss Sullivan."

"Good day," she said and watched as he whirled around and all but stomped out of the building.

Smiling, she stood there stunned. She had a bakery. A business of her own.

Abigail came around the corner, grinning. "You got the bakery."

"Yes, but the son is not too happy."

Laughing they walked towards the back. "Now, when will the girls arrive to help me, because he's going to do everything he can to make this bakery fail. I just know it."

Chapter Four

Luca walked into the bright sunshine and stared up and down the streets of New Hope. His dream had been within his grasp when suddenly it was snatched from him, all because of that petite girl. He'd never felt so angry in all his life and yet the pint-sized woman had stood up to him. She had not backed down.

But he couldn't let her lease the bakery forever, and yet, all she and his father had done was make him doubt his decisions. He needed the money for the vineyard and yet the family bakery held so many good memories.

Yet, if he were to open it again, his father would be there working harder than ever. As it was, he would have to watch him carefully not to let him spend too much time with Bella.

He'd yelled her name in the mercantile and she hadn't told him he was being disrespectful, but she had given him just as good as he gave her. No woman had ever done that to him. Most of them when he raised his voice quaked with fear and scurried away like a frightened mouse.

And who were these suffragettes? Who did she think was going to help her make this bakery a success? Six weeks. In six weeks, he could move forward with the sale and eventually the vineyard.

Walking over to the lawyer's office, he knew he had to somehow convince the man to wait on the sale. As he opened the door, he took a deep breath and prayed the man would be patient.

"May I speak to Mr. Barton?"

"Just a minute," the young man sitting out front said. He knocked on the door that separated the man's office and then disappeared inside.

Luca didn't really like Mr. Barton. He was a domineering, haughty man who was pompous and contemptuous. But he'd had the best offer.

In less than a minute, he came back out. "Mr. Barton will see you."

Luca removed his hat and stepped inside the office.

A framed portrait of the man that Luca knew was Barton's great-grandfather hung on the wall behind his desk. Tim's family were the original settlers of New Hope and Tim Barton didn't hesitate to tell you how his granddaddy wouldn't have liked the fact that women now owned businesses. So Luca knew he would not be pleased to hear that his father had insisted that Bella be given a chance with the bakery.

"Hi, Luca. Have a seat."

Luca sank down into the leather chair across from the older man, hating the way the chair made him lower than Tim. He liked using his height to his advantage.

"I'm working on finalizing the paperwork over the sale of the bakery. We should be ready to wind up this deal in a couple of days," he said.

Why did the timing just seem off on everything about this sale? If this had been just a few days later, the building would have already sold.

"We have a problem," Luca said. "My father is not ready to sell the bakery."

"I thought you said he wanted to sell."

"He did. Until he lost the baking competition the other day. Now he has befriended Miss Sullivan and has decided to give her six weeks to make the bakery profitable."

Tim sighed and tilted his head. "Six weeks? That's all?"

"Yes," Luca said.

Tim laughed. "And if she's not profitable, he'll go through with the sale?"

God forbid that the woman actually made a profit because then his father would refuse to let him sell the building. And Bella would only be leasing, not purchasing the bakery.

"That's what he's saying."

A grin spread across Tim's face. "She's a woman. She knows nothing about business. This isn't a problem. It's more of a delay than I wanted, but..." he shrugged his shoulders. "In six weeks, she'll be worn out, broke, and the bakery will be mine."

Luca bit his lip wondering if he should warn the man about Bella's friends coming to town to help her. While he didn't think she could do this on her own, with other women helping, it could be possible. But she didn't have the business experience his mother and father had. Still he would be dishonest if he didn't tell Mr. Barton about the possible help coming to town.

"Well, there's one more thing," Luca said.

"What?"

"She mentioned something about some suffragettes coming to town to help her."

Tim Barton jumped up from his chair. "Over my cold, dead, body are we having a bunch of man-hating, controlling harlots coming into town."

"They're on their way."

That had certainly gotten a strong reaction from the autocratic man.

"And the sheriff needs to make certain they get right back on the next stage out of town. Those women want to take away our manhood. They would make us all eunuchs if we let them take control. No, siree, no woman I know is going to tell me what to do or she'll find herself staring up at me from the ground."

Luca wasn't exactly certain what the big deal about these women could be. But the idea of a man hitting a woman curled his toes, leaving him nauseous. No one should hit a woman. And he better never see this idiot strike a woman or he'd defend her himself.

He could understand why women would want to have control over their livelihood and not be at the mercy of depending on a man to take care of them. But he knew from past experience that Tim Barton had wanted Abigail Vanderhooten run out of town after her father died and she inherited his mercantile. Now he could be challenging Bella Sullivan to keep her from operating the bakery and her friends from arriving.

"Don't worry about the sale. We just need to make certain Miss Sullivan is not successful, and that her misguided women friends are sent packing as soon as they arrive. Now excuse me, but I need to visit the sheriff and make him aware of what's about to hit New Hope."

Luca watched as the man walked out of the office and heard the door slam. He'd never been too fond of Tim Barton, but now he just thought he was a rude, obnoxious bore.

~

The next day, Bella had her head in her new bakery's oven, scrubbing the brick walls, her apron had smudges of dirt smeared on the cloth and her hair was falling loose in strands from the top of her hair. She'd tried to put it up, but the curls refused to stay in place in the heat and humidity of Texas.

The bakery was really in great shape. It was cleaner than she'd expected and Abigail had already ordered in extra flour and sugar. Within a day, she hoped to have her first batch of bread in the oven rising and another batch baking.

She would do twelve loaves the first day and they were first come, first sold, unless her clients signed up for her to bake them their own special loaf and have it available on a certain day at a specific time.

She was going to do everything she could to make this successful if it killed her, or she'd have to go home to St. Louis. Where she knew there would be a stranger waiting for her to marry.

Abigail was getting married soon and she didn't want to interfere with the newlyweds. She wanted to ask Franco about the apartment upstairs. It would be so convenient.

Crawling deeper into the oven, her backside bent over and vulnerable, she heard a deep voice behind her.

"Ciao."

She hit her head on the top of the oven. "Oww."

Backing out, she turned to stare at Luca, so cool and confident standing in the doorway. "Sorry, to disturb you. I thought maybe I would come by and see how well you're doing."

What was he doing here? Especially after their disagreement the day before when he'd made it clear to her that he didn't want her in the bakery.

"I'm trying to get the bakery ready to open the day after tomorrow."

"Looks good." He nodded. "I also came by to apologize for how I acted yesterday. I was upset that Papa wanted to reopen the bakery that almost killed him."

She nodded, hoping that was the end of it and he would leave. She still had a lot of things to do. "Fair enough, apology accepted."

"I also wanted to see if there was anything I could do to help you."

She frowned. Now she was getting suspicious. Why would he be so nice after he'd argued so hard for her not to have the bakery? "Okay, now you're crossing the line. I could accept your apology, but I can't accept you helping me."

He grinned. "It is my penance. Papa was not happy when I told him I had spoken to you."

Laughing, she could just see the elder Mr. Ruffini upset with what his son had said. The thought of Franco requiring his son to come help her was sweet, but she would rather he just came on his own. She had to stop thinking of this man in ways beyond an acquaintance.

"Later, I should have a wagon that needs unloading, but until then, I'm almost finished here. You can help me fire up the ovens."

He smiled at her and shrugged his shoulders. "Let me help you get them started. The reason this building is off away from the others is because of these ovens. They must be watched closely or they can catch the building on fire. It's why Papa built the apartment over the bakery. This way, he would be close."

All afternoon she'd thought about the apartment and wondered if she could use that as well. This way she and the suffragettes could get away from Abigail and Jack after the wedding.

"I would like to use that apartment," she said. "Abigail and Jack are soon going to marry and well..." she glanced at him shyly. "I think they could use some time without a house guest."

Nodding, he said, "Of course."

"Thank you, I'll move in tomorrow. Not that I have a lot."

"It's furnished. You can just use the furniture that's there."

"Thank you," she said, her heart warming. Why was he being so helpful? She couldn't help but think there must be a reason for his sudden change of heart.

"Did you tell the buyer that he would have to wait?" she asked, watching him as he moved to the woodpile and began to place wood in the cold ovens. She knew it would be a lot of work to keep the bakery going, but she could hardly wait to spend time manipulating the dough and baking it in the wood fired oven.

"Yes, I spoke to him. He's agreed to wait," he said, striking a match and lighting the kindling.

"Is that why you're being so helpful?" she asked.

He shrugged. "Let's just say it helps."

She gazed at his dark hair, his high cheekbones and felt an incredible urge to swipe the curl that kept falling onto his face away from his eyes. "As much as you want to hate me for keeping you from selling this place, I am extremely grateful to you and your father."

"I don't hate you." He looked around the bakery. "I know Papa thinks I dislike being here, but that's not true. My fondest memories are of being here with him and Mama. It's hard riding by, seeing the lamps lit and knowing it's not them working inside."

A twinge of heartache gripped her. She could understand why seeing someone else in the place where they had great memories would be difficult.

"But I want to take the family business in a new direction and need the cash from the sale. Without that money, it will be a lot harder to get started."

What was he doing that he needed the money? He'd not said what he wanted to do. His words made her feel uneasy, but then again, his father had made the decision she could lease the bakery from him.

Tilting her head she stared at him as he lit the flames. The fire roared in the oven. She couldn't contain her smile. "It's going."

"Yes, you can start baking in there tomorrow."

She reached out and grabbed his hand. At the feel of his skin beneath her fingers, her heart raced and her chest tightened. "Thank you."

He smiled and pulled her towards him. His other hand reached out and touched her cheekbone and she gazed up at him, wanting him to kiss her.

How could she in fewer than twenty-four hours go from almost hating Luca to wanting his lips on hers? No, she hadn't hated him. She'd just been so frustrated that he would think she had deceived his father in some way.

"I really didn't persuade your father to keep the bakery. He offered it to me." She licked her lips nervously.

His hands reached out and cupped her face as he pulled her closer. "I know."

His lips moved toward her as her heart rate accelerated. When their mouths touched, she sighed and sank into his arms like she'd come home. His mouth plundered hers as he kissed her like no man had ever before.

He sought the edges of her lips, gently nipping her until she opened for him and his tongue swept inside her mouth, shocking her. Like no kiss she'd ever experienced before heat began to infuse her from the bottoms of her toes, raging like a forest fire in her center, leaving her limbs limp.

Though her experiences with kisses were limited, no man had ever kissed her like he wanted to consume her, weakening her resistance. His mouth felt heavenly against her own. She wound her arms up and around his neck. He pressed her against his chest and she felt her breasts smashed against his rock solid muscles. She moaned deep in her throat.

Suddenly the door to the bakery slammed open, women giggling loudly as they entered the bakery. Then they went silent.

"Who's that?" someone said.

"Luca Ruffini, the owner," Abigail whispered.

She pulled out of his arms, her breathing harsh as they turned to stare at the silent women who stood in the door watching them. Dear God, the suffragettes had arrived just in time to see her experiencing the hottest kiss of her life.

"Well, it looks to me like she's getting along just fine with the owner of the bakery," Diamond, the toughest of the group said.

~

After Luca left, Abigail walked over to Bella and smiled. "I think we came at a bad time."

She shook her head. "Oh no, you came at the perfect time."

"But we interrupted him kissing you. And that is one handsome Italian," Diamond said, nodding. "Does he have any brothers?"

Bella tried very hard not to smile, wanting to savor that moment and hold it close for a while. Luca Ruffini's mouth was a dangerous weapon and she couldn't help but think she wanted more.

"His brother is sixteen." Bella turned to the group. "Have I told you hello and how nice it is to see you here?"

They all laughed and Bella hugged each girl. She was so excited to see Callie, Diamond, and Georgia. Only months had passed since she'd last seen them, but it felt more like years.

"Where are the others?" she asked.

"Faith couldn't come and Haley may show up eventually, I sent her a letter to let her know where we are," Callie said.

They had all been such close friends while they attended the university and lived in the same dorm. But not one of them had graduated from college and now Bella wasn't certain they would.

"Emma is in medical school. She's determined to become a doctor," Georgia responded.

"We came to help you clean," Diamond said. "Not that I really want to clean a brick oven."

Bella shook her head. "The oven is already cleaned. But the best news, ladies, is that Luca told me we can all stay in the apartment upstairs over the bakery."

Abigail frowned. "You're no longer going to stay with me?"

Bella hugged her friend close. She'd been afraid that Abigail would have her feelings hurt if they didn't all stay with her, but it was better if she and Jack had time alone. "You're soon to be married, and I think you and that good-looking husband-to-be of yours would like some alone time."

Abigail blushed. "But..."

The girls giggled. Bella didn't want to think of all of them changing from this moment in time. Abigail would soon be married and not long afterward possibly a mother. It just seemed so quick, but it was the circle of life.

"Yes, I can just see the man living with five women and trying to have sex with his bride. Not a good way to start a marriage," Bella replied.

"Girls," Abigail said. "I didn't think we'd do it the first night. Maybe I'm being naive, but I thought we'd wait."

All of the women laughed out loud.

"You think that man of yours is going to wait another day?" Diamond said, shaking her red curls. "You're wrong. That man is going to expect his just desserts as soon as nightfall arrives. You've had him hanging on now for several months. We've arrived, it's time to set the date."

Abigail smiled. "Well, we were thinking six weeks from this Saturday, if that was agreeable with Bella. I want you to bake the wedding cake."

What an honor. To bake her friend's wedding cake and serve it to the people of New Hope. If it was successful, she would receive even more orders for cakes in the future.

Squeals of laughter sounded from the women as they gathered around Bella and Abigail. "I'm delighted you asked me to bake your cake. Thrilled in fact. Thank you."

Bella hugged Abigail thinking that she was closer to this woman who had taken her in when she needed a place to hide than even her own sister.

"Oh my goodness," Bella said releasing Abigail and wiping the tears leaking from her eyes. "What a night. The best kiss I've ever experienced, my best friend wants me to bake her wedding cake, and all of you show up. This day just can't get any better."

And that kiss had been hotter than a fireplace on a snowy day. She'd felt like she'd go up in flames and would welcome the blaze. Luca Ruffini had melted her clear to her toes and she didn't know if that was a good thing or a bad one at the moment.

"Yes, it can," Diamond said. "We need to celebrate everyone's happiness and success. And to new beginnings."

Bella believed that Diamond was hiding a past, but she had no way of knowing for certain and she loved her friend too much to ask. Even if the girl was hiding something, they loved her unconditionally.

"Let's go to Abigail's and drink wine and catch up. Tomorrow we can clean the apartment and move in. But tonight, let's celebrate," Bella said, taking her apron off and laying it on the counter. She put the door up on the oven so the fire would hopefully burn most of the night, heating the bricks. Tomorrow she would begin the baking.

Opening the door, they spilled out onto the wooden sidewalks. As they strolled toward the mercantile, they could hear the music from the saloon, echoing down the street. A man's eyes widened as he passed them on the street. "Good evening, ladies."

"Evening," they chorused and then giggled.

"Yes, the men in this town will think you girls are answers to their prayers. New meat just arrived in town," Abigail said. "Be careful."

Sometimes Bella felt sorry for the lonely men who so desperately wanted a wife and family, and then other times, she couldn't help but think there was a reason why they'd never found anyone to marry them. A reason she didn't want to know.

Diamond shook her head. "I'm not searching for a husband. I'm looking for a new start. A job or a business to run."

"Me, too," Callie said.

Georgia sighed. "I don't know. Maybe a man would be easier than trying to change the world. At least maybe I could bend him to my will."

A snort sounded from Abigail. "Don't count on it.

Suddenly, the sheriff stepped in front of them. "Ladies."

Bella's heart thudded in her chest at the expression on the man's face. Oh no, this could mean trouble and she'd already seen the inside of a jail with these women. She wasn't ready to experience that cold, damp, place again.

Abigail moved to stand before the man. "Yes, Sheriff?"

"You know, New Hope is a quiet little frontier town or at least it was up until Miss Vanderhooten returned home. Are you ladies the suffragettes?"

"Yes," they all responded including Abigail.

"When I was told of your impending arrival, one of our elected officials suggested I should just load you girls up and put you on the next stage going out of town. But I assured the man, you have nothing to fear from a group of women. Because these ladies are not going to cause me any trouble in any way. Are you, ladies?"

Diamond snorted. "Depends."

Abigail laid her hand on Diamond. "Now, Sheriff, I know you're just doing your job, but we don't want trouble. We just want to be able to live our lives like all God-fearing people do."

Bella could guess who the troublemaking elected official was who had warned the sheriff. None other than Mr. Barton, a man who could not help but stick his nose in everyone's town business. If you needed to know something, go see Mr. Barton. He could give you anyone who lived in New Hope their history.

He nodded. "I want you girls to know I went out on a limb for you. I told this person the men in this town were looking for good women to become their wives and you girls could be the answer to their prayers.

"But I'm not going to put up with any shenanigans you ladies may be thinking of pulling. If you want to stay, that's great, but there won't be any marching or any fighting or any other tomfoolery. Do you understand?"

No one said anything. They only stared at him. Bella knew that could mean trouble if they decided they weren't happy with something going on in town. She'd seen her friends fly into action and show their freedom of speech.

"Well, it was nice meeting you and having this little chat. Enjoy your evening," he said and started to walk off.

Abigail laid her hand on his arm. "Tell Mr. Barton these girls have arrived to bring new businesses and new opportunities to New Hope." She smiled up at him. "Female commerce at its finest."

The sheriff frowned and shook his head. "Well, that will certainly get him riled, won't it?"

The women laughed.

"New Hope is leading the way toward the nineteenth century where women will be just as equal as a man," Bella said quietly.

"You ladies have a good evening," the sheriff said looking worried as he hurried away.

Bella watched him leave thinking this town would never be the same.

Chapter Five

Luca walked into the house, dropping his saddle bags by the door. His sister came around the corner and glanced at him.

Maybe talking to his sister would help. He felt rattled, unsure of what he was feeling. That kiss had been almost explosive.

"You're late. Papa has already gone to bed. I was just about to go up myself."

"Yeah, I stopped by the bakery and apologized to Bella this evening."

His sister smiled. "That was nice. I can't wait to try her bread and see if it's any good."

He nodded remembering the feel of her lips against his own. He hadn't expected to experience such a reaction to her kiss. Sure, he had kissed many girls, but none of them affected him like kissing this woman.

If her friends had not walked in, there was no telling what could have happened. He wanted nothing more than to lean her over one of the tables in the bakery and have his way with her right there in front of the windows. At that moment, he didn't care about anything but her.

"What's wrong?" she asked. "I can tell something is bothering you."

"I made a mistake tonight." The words slipped out before he could stop them. His sister picked up on his emotions better than his brother or father. She understood him better than anyone in the family except for his dear departed mother.

"Another mistake? What happened?"

Sighing, he walked over to a chair and sat. She sank onto the sofa next to him. "I don't know why I did it. One moment, we were talking and the next, I was pulling her to me and kissing her. I had no intention of doing something so foolish, but once I did, now I want to kiss her again."

His sister giggled. "Maybe she is the one who will win your cuore."

His stomach clenched with fear as he thought about Bella. He wasn't ready to give anyone his heart, but especially not her. Right now, he wanted to get his vineyard going before he thought of marriage and love. "It was just a mistaken moment of weakness. I won't let it happen again."

His sister, ever the romantic, refused to let it go. "Did you enjoy kissing her?"

His brows drew together in a frown as he glared at her. "That is none of your business."

"Well, you must have thought about it all the way home."

Of course, the memory of the rush of passion he'd felt lingered with him. He'd hurried out of the bakery with five women standing around staring at him. But holding Bella in his arms, his skin touching hers and his mouth dreaming of kissing her once again overwhelmed him. He hadn't expected to feel so much from just the taste of her mouth.

"It was a kiss, nothing more," he said with determination. "I will make certain it doesn't happen again. Now, don't you think you should go to bed?"

But how could he guarantee he wouldn't kiss her again when already his body and his soul wanted to touch her lips to his once again. In fact, he couldn't wait to taste her and hold her in his arms.

She stood and laughed. "Mama always told me that when the right man comes into my life that his kiss will melt my bones, but his heart will show me he is the man for me. Any man or woman who loves you will put your needs above their own, and that will show you their heart."

"Now is not the right time for love. I don't need the responsibilities of a wife. After the vineyard is running smoothly, then I will consider love and marriage. But not now."

There was so much he needed to do with the vineyard and she held the keys to the bakery. And he feared how this was all going to end. One of them was not going to be happy.

"Maybe, but sometimes we don't have control over when is the right time for us to meet the love of our lives. Goodnight, Luca."

He watched as his sister walked up the stairs, leaving him sitting in front of the fireplace. Bella was nice, but what did he really know about this woman? All he knew was she liked to bake, wanted his family's bakery, and could kiss like an angel.

Where did she come from and who was her family? And did all that really matter, when all he had to do was glance at her full, ripe lips and he wanted to block the world out and kiss her until they were both satisfied?

~

The next morning, Bella was mixing the dough for her first batch of bread when the door to the bakery opened and Franco walked in.

"Good morning," he said, glancing around at the changes she had made. The counters were empty, but the tables where people could sit and talk had new tablecloths with vases of fresh roses in them. "Looking good."

"Good morning, Mr. Ruffini," she called. "I'm making the first batch of bread now. Come on back to the kitchen."

He walked past the counter and entered the kitchen in the back. He took a deep breath. "Oh, how I have missed this place. I use to love to be upstairs in the apartment when Maria was baking bread. The smells would drift upstairs and it was all I could do to keep from running downstairs and grabbing the olive oil."

There was something almost heavenly about the smell of fresh bread. The aroma had her taste buds watering with anticipation.

Bella smiled at him and he watched her carefully as she kneaded the dough. "I have two loaves close to the oven, rising and another two about ready to start."

He opened the door to the brick oven. "The oven is still too warm. Give it at least another ten minutes. If not, the bread will be too crunchy on the outside."

There was so much to learn about the way the brick ovens controlled the heat. Little things that could mean the difference between a good loaf of bread or a crusty, dry loaf.

"Thank you. How long did it take you to learn the oven?"

Glancing at her he said, "My mother, she baked in a brick oven, so I've known since I was a kid. But you will soon learn as well."

"My father's kitchen has one of those new ceramic ovens. It took our cook some time to learn how to use it. She burned my father's dinner many times."

Nodding, he watched as she kneaded the dough as she had for many years. There was something about the texture between her fingers as she rolled the dough in the bowl. It was almost soothing.

"That's enough," he said gazing at her. "It's ready to be placed on the rack to rise."

"Rack?" she asked wondering what he was talking about. There were so many small details still to learn.

"Yes," he said glancing around the kitchen. "I made special racks for the dough to sit on and rise before it went into the oven."

Opening cabinets, he finally found what he was searching for. "Ah, here." He took the metal pans out and slid them into place near the oven. "See?"

"That's smart. Now I can just slide the bread into the oven."

"Yes," he said. "Let me make the next loaves."

She smiled as she took her dough and placed it in the pans. "As long as your son doesn't get angry with me again."

"Luca is protective of his family. He is going to be a great man."

"He came by and apologized last night."

"He did? For what?"

She thought for sure Franco knew about their disagreement and now she wished she hadn't said anything. "He thought I approached you about leasing the bakery after he had told me no. So when you suggested I run the bakery, he thought I was behind your request."

Franco laughed. "Fate works in mysterious ways. You wanted the bakery, and I wanted you to have the place, but Luca, he is still learning that fate will have her way."

Bella smiled, a feeling of contentment coming over her. She hadn't thought of it that way. "Anyway, he apologized because we raised our voices to each other."

"That's good."

"What do you mean that's good. People should get along."

"Yes, they should. But sometimes the passion, it gets in the way. You felt passionate about the bakery and he feels passionate about the vineyard. It makes me smile."

What in the world was he talking about? Yes, she cared about the bakery, but the vineyard. Was that the special project Luca referred to when he said he needed the sale of the bakery? What did the two have to do with one another?

"My son is a good man and he's not hard on the eyes either. And he's a Ruffini. We're a good family, full of love for one another."

Did he think she was applying to be a member? All his words accomplished was to remind her that her own family was in turmoil. Her father and mother didn't love one another and she'd seen her father out on the town with another woman before she left for college. There was just so much that wasn't right with them and she didn't know how to fix the problems.

"You must miss your wife terribly."

"I think of her every day, almost every moment. She was my cuore."

Bella frowned. "What is cuore."

He laughed at her pronunciation. "It's Italian for heart. She was my life, my love, my very soul."

Bella felt tears well up at the way he talked about the woman he still loved. She'd never heard her father say he loved her mother.

"What about your family? Why are you not living with your mama and papa? They must be worried about you."

Oh, they probably were, but she was not going to stay in St. Louis and be paraded through society for the highest bidder. She would never marry unless it was for love and she didn't care how many rich, socialite bachelors her father presented.

"My family is not from around here. My father wants me to marry, and I refuse."

That was a fast, simple explanation of what was wrong with her family. But there was a much deeper core.

"Why? That is every father's wish for his daughter to marry well, so he doesn't have to worry about her and knows she's being taken care of."

"Well, it's not what I want."

"You don't want a bambino? A family of your own? A man to hold you in his arms and tell you he loves you?" Franco asked, mixing yeast into the flour, glancing at her, his eyes darkening.

Of course, she did, but she wanted more. Why was it that women could not have more than just a family? And why did she have to settle for who her father wanted her to marry?

"Yes, I want a family of my own, a man who loves me, but I love the baking, the creating something with my own hands. Of being in charge of my own shop. This means so much to me."

He smiled, his brows rising. "The flour, it is in your blood. Of course, you want to create. And you shall."

She didn't know if the flour was in her blood, but she loved to bake, and here she was the happiest. Working, here in the kitchen, selling her goods.

"But if I stayed with my family, I would have been forced to marry a man I didn't love. I want more."

That didn't mean she didn't love her family. She missed them and hoped that someday they could reunite and would accept her decision to create something out of her life besides being a rich socialite who held tea parties all day.

"Fathers want what is best for their children. My daughter is a beauty and I hope she finds a man who is worthy of her love. And the same for my sons. I want them to marry women who are passionate about them. But you must also be strong individuals who are happy before you can come together as a couple. My Luca is close. He must learn the lesson of love and passion, but I think he's ready."

Bella felt her heart sort of skip a beat. He'd certainly been very capable last night when he'd kissed her. She still grew warm thinking of how she'd melted into his arms and the way his lips had done such incredible things to her mouth. The way he'd completely melded her mouth to his. The man certainly knew how to kiss.

"Aha," Franco said. "These two loaves are ready to rise. May I show you how to make shortbread cookies the children love?"

"Please," she said. "I need more items in the display case."

He smiled. "Oh, my Bella, I think you are going to be perfect for the bakery."

Grinning, she gazed at Franco. "I hope so. I really like it here and I'm thrilled to be baking with you."

And his son wasn't too bad either. But whether or not that kiss had a future, she didn't know. But she did know she would like to try his luscious mouth once again and have a second taste to determine if she liked it as much the second time around.

~

Franco almost danced into the house after spending the better part of the day with Bella in the bakery. The girl was a delight and he knew she would fit into the family perfectly. But he had to be careful and not show his son too much interest or the boy would run.

His daughter glanced up from the supper she was fixing in the kitchen. "Papa. You're home. I've been worried."

He grinned and thought of the day cooking and preparing for the reopening of the bakery he'd loved.

"I spent the day in the bakery with Bella."

Grinning widely, his daughter said, "And?"

He put his thumb and first finger together and brought it to his mouth, kissed them and released. She nodded in understanding. "I thought so as well. I'm going to run by the bakery tomorrow when I'm in town and speak to her."

"Don't say anything to your brother or her."

Laughing she stirred the sauce. "I won't. Now, wash up, it's time to eat. And find the boys and tell them supper is ready."

Quickly, he went into his bedroom and washed. Looking at the bed, he missed his wife once again. She was gone, the bakery was being handled by someone new and their oldest son...was now the head of the family business. Life changes and he was doing his best to go along.

Walking out the door, he saw his sons were seated at the dinner table. He took his place at the head and then turned to Luca. "Son, will you please say the blessing."

After the prayer was said, they began to pass the food. "Thank you for cooking, Cara."

"You're welcome, Papa."

"How was the bakery?" Luca asked. "I saw you were there when I went into town."

There was so much he wanted to say, but somehow he had to play it very cool and detached. If Luca even suspected he was happy and wanted Bella as his daughter-in-law, he would flee and probably sell the bakery right away.

"Bella was cooking her first loaves of bread in the oven, and then I showed her how to make the shortbread cookies we all enjoy so much. She has much to learn." He shook his head. "In such a short time."

He felt like a fisherman dangling a worm in front of a fish, hoping it would bite. Would Luca take the bite and go for the worm?

"Now, Papa, don't start asking for more time."

"I'm not. I think she is going to really put everything she has into making the bakery a success. She's an innocent, sweet, young woman, and I hope you'll stay away from her so she can work to make the bakery a success. She needs to learn how to express love with the flour. Make the bread so good, it sells itself."

He'd said enough, now he needed to sit back and wait.

Luca held his fork in midair. "Why would you think that I would try to stop her? I said she has six weeks to make it a success."

"No reason. But she's a beautiful, young flower, and you're an Italian boy who likes pretty women. Just don't go sniffing in this garden."

Luca shook his head and laughed. "I'm too busy playing amongst the grapevines, preparing them for winter. I don't have time to stop and smell the roses."

Franco nodded his approval. "Good. Then Bella can concentrate on improving her craft and returning the bakery to its former glory. I'm going to help her as much as I can. But her focus must be on learning to craft the bread."

"See, there is no reason for me to be in the bakery because I know you will be there," Luca said, not glancing at his father.

Franco saw his daughter watching the two of them. She knew what he was doing and she was doing her best to keep a smile from appearing on her face. She also knew he could never use this tactic on her because she would be aware of how he goaded her brother into courting Bella.

Now if only his plan would work, he would have a new daughter, his bakery back, and hopefully soon, some grand bambinos.

~

Luca watched his father go to bed. He sat in the family room of the small ranch house. Had Bella told his father that he kissed her last night? Had Cara leaked his weak moment? Or was his father just a wily old man trying to hang onto the place he'd spent most of his adult life and wasn't ready to let go?

He sighed and leaned back against the horsehair sofa. If his mother was here, he could discuss the feelings that swirled around when he thought of the dark-haired beauty. But she was long gone and his sister had already retired for the evening. His brother was much too young to share tales of women with.

But if his father was just trying to hang onto the bakery, then Luca would need to do everything possible to make Bella fail. He didn't want to hurt the girl. She seemed nice and he liked her, but his own dreams were at stake and his father's health to consider.

He didn't want his papa to be working the long hours in the bakery every day. He would throw one grand fit if his father thought he was helping this girl for long periods of time. After the incapacitating stroke, they'd all nursed Papa back to health and now he wanted to work again.

Yet, he needed his own dreams to succeed and if that meant the bakery could not make a profit, he would do everything he could to ensure that it wasn't successful.

So tomorrow, he would begin to woo the young woman. And that wouldn't be difficult at all. For the kiss they'd shared the other night certainly showed how much spark and passion there was between them. The woman certainly smelled like heaven and kissed like Satan.

Chapter Six

Opening day, Bella sent her friends into the street with baskets of sample slices of bread. She hoped to entice her customers to come to the store, knowing certain people in town would do everything they could to see she wasn't successful.

Especially one Tim Barton who thought good Christian women walked behind their husbands and spoke only when spoken to. But Bella knew her friends would never let a man rule them and wanted to be seen as equals, as partners in a marriage. She wondered if they weren't all, but Abigail, doomed to being spinsters.

The image of Luca came to mind, and she smiled remembering the kiss he'd given her. She hadn't seen him since that night and hoped he would come by for the opening. So far she'd only had one customer today, but it was early still and she knew the day was young.

The door opened and Franco came in. "Good morning, beautiful Bella. How are you this fine morning?"

She smiled. The old man was always so happy, so jolly that he was a joy to be around. No matter what happened with the bakery, she hoped they would remain friends. "I'm doing well, and you?"

He glanced around the empty bakery and spread his hands out wide. "I see no customers."

Her heart jumped a little, hoping this didn't mean what she feared. What if Mr. Barton managed to keep most of the townspeople away? "It's early. My friends are walking up and down Main Street handing out bread samples. Abigail has a flyer up in her store announcing the grand opening and the newspaper is going to run an ad."

Franco's hand swiped at the air. "Word of mouth will bring you customers. Just you wait and see."

"I hope you're right."

Just then Diamond came running back into the bakery, her basket empty. "That Tim Barton is the most despicable man I've ever met. Do you know he dumped my basket out into the street? Told me I was a sinful woman and for me to take the next stage out of town."

"Oh no," Bella said, feeling bad her friend had been accosted by the meanest man in town. "Are you all right?"

This type of harassment was exactly what she feared Tim Barton would do, and she hoped her friends were capable of standing up to the ignorant man.

"I'm fine. I told him I'd handled men worse than him and if he wanted to see how sinful I could be, come to the bakery."

Bella started laughing, but Franco didn't smile and appeared angry.

"He is, how do you say in English...small minded."

"Give me more samples and I'll head back out. Any customers yet?"

Bella sighed. "Just one, Mrs. Jackson."

"She used to come in all the time. She's a great customer," Franco said.

"Maybe you should make some of those peach turnovers that won you the bake off."

Bella turned to Franco an idea popping into her head. "We talked about having another bake off. Maybe we should do it now?"

She didn't know if she could beat the old man a second time. Somehow, she felt like the moon and stars had just aligned on her side that day.

Franco smiled, his eyes twinkling like a little kid. "I bake my Castagnole and you bake your peach turnovers. We have a ballot box and people in town can choose which one they like the best."

"Yes," Bella said smiling.

"Oh, that sounds like so much fun," Diamond said. "And it would drive customers into the bakery."

"Diamond, tell everyone you meet about the contest. It begins Saturday at noon and goes until five. Franco and I square off against one another again."

If they could get the town involved, it would be so much fun. And a great reason for everyone to come into the bakery, vote, and purchase bread.

"Yes, ma'am. I'll tell Abigail to put up a notice in the store."

"Maybe this will bring us customers."

Later that evening as Bella closed the bakery, Diamond counted the cash. "Well, I guess, the day ended better than expected. You made nine dollars."

"Not bad, but I was hoping it would be better," Bella said, putting dough on the shelf to rise. Before she went home tonight, she wanted to bake at least four more loaves of fresh bread and also prepare the dough for her peach turnovers.

Diamond stood. "How long are you planning on staying here tonight?"

"Oh, about another hour and I'll be done."

"Don't work too much longer. You've got a big day tomorrow and you're going to be up at the crack of dawn."

Bella smiled at her friend. "Thank you for helping me today. I'm so glad you all came to Texas."

She was beginning to understand what Luca was saying about the bakery and how she couldn't do it alone. Thank goodness her friends were here and helping. She owed them so much and hoped to someday repay their kindness.

"Yeah, so far I've liked this little town, except for that guy. I even had three men offer to buy me dinner. I turned them all down, told them I was too busy helping my friends. But in Boston, I never felt accepted. Here the men are happy to see me."

In Boston, Diamond had worked at a bar to support herself while she attended the university. Originally from New York, her mother had named her Diamond because that was her favorite piece of jewelry from her gentleman friends. She didn't talk much about her past, only to say her mother was an actress.

"You're beautiful, Diamond."

"Well, in Boston, you had to be beautiful and have the right family name before most men would accept you."

While Bella had enjoyed living and going to school in Boston, society had been very snooty even for a rich girl like her. It had been hard to find acceptance.

Bella slid the loaves of bread in the oven. "Now for the turnovers."

"I think I'm going upstairs and help Callie finish cleaning the apartment."

"Okay, I won't be long."

Diamond disappeared up the stairs, leaving Bella alone. She hummed a tune as she made the dough for her favorite dessert. Her hands were deep in the flour when the bell above the door tinkled. "Come in."

She hoped it wasn't a thief as she was hardly in a position to protect herself. She craned her neck behind her and saw Luca standing in the frame. "Come back to the kitchen."

"Hello," he said. "How did your first day go."

"Great," she lied. She was not about to tell him sales had been disappointing, to say the least.

"Good," he said. "I just don't want you to be discouraged if the bakery doesn't do well."

She wanted to tell him not to worry, that she still had some tricks up her sleeve, but decided to let it go. They were getting along and he was being kind.

"I won't," she lied already knowing she wasn't happy with today's sales and hoped that the bake off brought in more clients.

Suddenly her sleeve that had been rolled up all day came down. Both of her hands were in the wet dough. "Could you do me a favor?"

"What?"

"Would you roll my sleeve back up? It's getting into the flour and it's not the flavor I'm looking for in my bread."

He walked up behind her. She could feel his presence so close and smell the manly scent of Luca. Her body seemed to vibrate and warmth spread through her. He reached out and rolled her sleeve back, his hands brushing against her skin. She glanced at him, her eyes widening at the feel of his fingers. She licked her lips and swallowed. Of all the times for her sleeve to come unraveled. "Thank you."

"You're welcome," he said staring at her and then glancing at the bowl. "Let me help you."

"What? Are your hands clean?"

While the words sounded strained to her ears, all she could think about was how he was standing so close behind her. If she leaned back, she would run smack into the hard muscles of his chest. And while that wouldn't be a bad thing, she needed to finish this bread.

"I washed them before I walked in."

His hands came around either side of her and dipped into the dough. "Papa said you should treat the dough like it's a woman and caress it gently and firmly."

"Oh my. But I am a woman," she said her voice little more than a whisper as the air in her lungs seemed to disappear, leaving her breathless.

He smiled. "Yes, I definitely noticed."

Her heart beat suddenly tripled at his words. His hands covered hers and together they massaged the dough, mixing and turning, their fingers entwined kneading the floury mixture. She didn't know what to do or say. All she knew was that with his arms wrapped around her, his hands helping her caress the raw bread, her mind filled with the memory of his lips on hers and she wanted that again. Just the thought of him caressing her had her breathing coming in a hitch.

"There, that should be enough kneading until the dough rises, then we will try again."

She didn't know if she could do it again without cooking the dough from the heat of her body, as a furnace seem to have inflamed her and her voice sounded strained. "Thank you."

Gently he turned her in his arms and his lips descended on hers. His mouth consumed her, engulfing her lips within his own, his tongue stroking her mouth. She leaned toward him, wanting to be closer to his body, his arms wrapping around her.

Without removing his lips, he moved the bowl of dough out of the way and lifted her onto her work-space. His flour encrusted hands reaching up to hold her face where she could not break the seal of his lips. His tongue swept into her mouth and she moaned in the back of her throat.

He was the enemy. He didn't want her to have the bakery, and yet, all she could think about was the way he made her feel. She wanted to continue this kiss until...whatever happened between a man and a woman occurred. She had no idea except what she'd heard whispered in school. But no one had ever mentioned how a kiss could make you heat from within. How it seemed to ignite a fire in your blood that raged with the need to be consumed.

Nibbling on her lips, she grasped him and slanted her lips for even more access to Luca and his incredible mouth.

"Bella," Callie yelled down the stairs. "How much longer are you going to be?"

Her eyes opened and she stared at him as they came apart.

"Bella?"

"Just a little longer," she said weakly.

"Are you okay?"

"Yes," she said her breath rushing from her body. She didn't need them to come down and realize what she'd been doing with Luca. "I'm just cleaning up."

She looked down at her dress, her apron and saw the smudges of flour and dough where his hands had touched her. She'd enjoyed his caresses and wanted more. She swiped her finger across Luca's cheek to remove dough and left behind a trail of flour. She giggled. "I think we're a mess."

He grinned. "Yes, we are."

Going to the sink, he grabbed a wet rag and brought it back. Gently, he wiped the white powder from her face. Then she took the rag he offered and began to wipe his face clean. "What are we doing, Luca?"

"I don't know," he said. "But I'm finding you hard to resist."

"And me you. But you want me to fail," she said.

"No, I want the bakery to fail," he responded quietly.

"What's the difference?"

"There is a huge difference. You can bake anywhere. The bakery I want closed for family reasons."

"But I need the bakery."

"And I need it closed."

They looked long and hard at one another and Bella felt regret. She liked Luca, but they wanted different things. He ran his hand through his hair, leaving a white streak of flour. She giggled and then reached up to dust it out.

"What if we don't talk about the success or failure of the bakery until my six weeks are up." She couldn't believe she was saying this. Offering him a chance to get to know her when she knew they would eventually fight over her dream.

His dark eyes grew large and he smiled. Reaching down, he kissed the top of her nose and then a quick swipe on the lips. "I like that idea. And since we're not going to discuss the closing of the bakery, why don't you go on a picnic with me tomorrow?"

"I can't. Your father and I are having a bake off tomorrow. But what if we go on Sunday when the bakery is closed."

He nodded. "I like that idea. I will take you after church."

He gripped her by the waist and slid her down to the floor. "I best be going before your friends come down and see what we've done."

"Yes, you should probably leave."

She walked him to the door. "Goodnight. Luca."

"Buona notte, fiera bellezza," he said softly and kissed her on the forehead as he walked out the door.

Her heart leaped into her throat at the sound of the Italian words. She didn't know what he said, but they warmed and made her feel special. She watched him go as she closed and locked the bakery. The man was dangerous and she couldn't seem to get enough of him. No man had ever made her feel like this. She couldn't wait until Sunday.

~

Saturday morning Franco and Bella stood behind the counter at the bakery, selling their deserts and watching the people in town cast their ballots. They had a steady stream of townsfolk and after they tasted the two pastries, they were buying bread and cookies and anything else Bella had prepared. They were selling the bread as fast as it came out of the ovens. And everyone would walk into the shop, take a deep breath and go aww...the smell of the yeast and sugar, a sweet inhalation.

At four o'clock, the crowds began to clear and the shelves were almost bare. They were out of cookies and the last loaves of bread had just gone into the oven. Everyone was exhausted, but joyous because they knew the event had been very successful. Franco had gone home to rest, tired and happy after spending most of the day helping her sell.

The bell above the door dinged and Bella looked up from the last loaves of bread she was sliding into the oven. Tim Barton strode into the room, a scowl on his face. He gazed around at the women standing behind the counter and at the display of turnovers and Castagnole. His lip curled into a snarl. "You are all harlots of the devil."

Diamond rolled her eyes and shook her head. "Well, if I'm a harlot, I'd like to know who I've been sleeping with."

Bella had to bite her lip to keep from snickering. The man was obsessed with women earning money and yet she was determined he was not going to ruin her day. "May I assist you, Mr. Barton? I'm just about sold out today, but I do have a couple of loaves of fresh bread if you're interested or you can sample the turnovers and the Castagnole and vote on which dessert and baker you prefer."

No matter how much he provoked her, she was not going to let him affect her. Today had been beyond glorious and sales had been brisk. She was happy and wanted to remain that way. And tomorrow she was going on a picnic with Luca.

He glared at her. "My great-grandfather built this town and he made it law that no woman should own a business. You have defiled his name, broken a biblical law, and riled the citizens in this town."

Bella glanced at her friends. "What did you girls do? Stand out in the streets and dance? That's against the law in New Hope. No dancing. I thought you were just handing out free samples of bread."

They giggled. "Do we have any sweet bread or cookies left you can give this man. I think he needs some sweets."

Callie shook her head. "We're starting businesses so we can take care of ourselves and not be dependent on a man. Is that so bad?"

"It's biblical that no woman shall own a business."

"Excuse me," quiet little Georgia said in her sweet southern voice. "My pappy was a preacher of the gospel. I was raised in the church and I don't remember that verse you're speaking of. And while men are to be head of the home, the woman plays an equal role as his helpmate and wife."

Bella stared at Georgia, learning something new about her friend. She was the quietest of the group and she'd never given them much information about her past. But she was a preacher's daughter.

"The law is the law," Tim said, his voice rising. "I will do my best to see you shut down."

"Just like you tried to shut Abigail down. I think that law was eradicated," Bella said quietly.

Bella had reached her limit. She was tired, she wanted to close the door on this man, but tried to be nice. Now she was ready for him to leave.

"She was the exception. It was not removed for new businesses," he said defiantly his voice rising.

Bella stared at him. "What does it matter? Am I taking business away from you? No. While I appreciate this friendly welcome call, if you're not going to purchase something, I have other customers who are waiting. I wish you well, Mr. Barton and hope that someday your daughter will not face the same barriers as women our age."

That was the wrong thing to say. His face turned red. She should never have mentioned his innocent daughter.

"My daughter will know her rightful place in this world. Married and taking care of her home and family," he said almost shouting.

Diamond opened the door of the bakery, giving him a hint it was time to go. "Well, good for her. Hope she marries a great man who will take care of her and she never has to try to raise her children alone or needs a bank account or has to earn a living."

Her words went right over his head.

"I will get you closed down. Just wait and see," he said and walked out the door.

After he left, the women all huddled together.

"Can he shut you down?" Georgia asked.

"I don't know. I'll talk to Abigail and Jack. He would know. But let's not let him ruin things. We've had an exceptional day today and I couldn't have done it without all of you."

"And now we are more determined than ever to make certain you're successful," Callie said, smiling at the group.

"To success," Georgia said and raised her hands in the air.

They all followed suit yelling success just as the next customer walked in the door.

"After this customer, let's count the votes and call it a day."

After they had counted the votes, Georgia smiled at Bella. "You won by two votes."

She frowned remembering how upset Franco had been when he lost. It was so close and the old man had helped her more than she could ever repay him. It was an easy decision. "No, Franco won."

"But Bella," Georgia said in her sweet southern drawl.

"After everything he's done for me, it's the least I can do."

Callie shook her head. "Franco will be happy."

~

Luca felt anxious as he drove the wagon toward the stream on the edge of town. The fall day was gorgeous, though the trees had yet to start changing colors. The air had turned cooler, but still summer refused to give up and change completely over to fall. The nights were still warm enough to leave the windows open and the days still needed a good breeze.

Bella sat next to him, her hip occasionally bumping against him as the wagon bounced on the road.

What was he doing? He liked this woman, and yet, here he was trying to stop her from making the bakery a success? Morally it felt wrong, and yet it would help him accomplish his dream. He needed the sale of that damn bakery if he was going to make the vineyard a success.

"I didn't see your father at church this morning," she said. "Is he okay?"

"He's fine. Just tired and I told him that he should stay home and rest today. No going to town. Strangely, he listened."

This woman was even watching over his father. His sister liked her, his father wanted him to stay away from her, and now he'd developed this fiendish plan to make her fail. It was wrong, but he was doing it.

"Is his health that bad?" she asked.

What could Luca say? After his mother died, his father had almost worn himself out. Luca had been wrong not to notice it before he actually collapsed. But even if he'd seen it coming, he didn't know if his father would have listened to him.

"When my mother took ill and eventually died, he buried his grief in working. He worked longer hours and took on even more of the baking. Everything mother had done, he did, plus running the business side of things.

"Eventually, he just wore himself completely out. He wasn't resting well at night and one day he collapsed. The doctor told him he had to slow down or he was going to die. I took over the bakery, and eventually, we made a family decision to close it and focus our interests on the vineyard."

"Vineyard? You haven't told me about the vineyard. You're growing grapes. For wine?"

He laughed and pulled the wagon to a halt beside a gurgling stream. Right now, the water was low as the heat of the summer had depleted the water. But soon the fall rains would come and it would once again be flowing at a high level.

Setting the brake on the wagon, he climbed down and then turned to help Bella alight. The feel of his hands touching her waist had his mind wandering in directions he shouldn't be going. He promised himself this picnic and the kisses before it were just to woo her away from the bakery. To divert her attention and help him to close the business.

Yet, his body wasn't responding like a disinterested suitor. Oh no, when he looked at Bella, he wanted to do more than kiss her. He wanted to touch her silky skin and explore her womanly curves. And that made him feel even more guilty.

Setting her on the ground, he reached in the back for the basket of food Cara had helped him prepare and the blanket.

"Let's find a spot along the creek," he said. Taking her by the hand, he led her to the creek's edge. "This should do."

They spread the blanket and then she sank onto the quilt. "Did your mother make this quilt?"

"No, it came from my grandmother who came over from Italy. There was a famine and her sister wrote to her and said come to America. She met my grandfather while she was here and never went back," he said, sitting down beside her. "Are you hungry?"

"Starving. Callie fried eggs for breakfast, and well, they were a little tough. We're trying to help her learn to cook."

He leaned back wondering how a woman didn't know how to cook. His sister had learned at a very young age and often made dinner for the family while they worked at the bakery. "How can she not know how to prepare food."

"Easy. When the servants do all the cooking, you never have to learn, until you no longer have servants and then you're on your own. Callie's family is wealthy," Bella said.

"I can't imagine," he replied, wondering if he could give up the cooking to a servant. But then again, when Cara had been ill or something had happened, he'd often stepped in and taken care of the meal for the family.

"Not everyone has a family like yours. I haven't met your brother, but you all seem to care about each other. Your father keeps telling me not to think too harshly of his son. That you have a good heart."

Luca smiled. "And do you think harshly of me?"

She laughed. "Only when we discuss the bakery, which we're not going to talk about today, remember."

Oh, the bakery, that evil thing between them that he wished he could solve somehow, but didn't know how to fix.

He leaned back on his elbows. "What about your family. Are they a loving group?"

She glanced at the river and sighed. "My mother is quiet and very withdrawn. My father makes all the decisions."

Luca stared at her. There was something odd about the way she spoke about the family who raised her. She had very little to say about them. She didn't gush about her people the way he would if he was describing his family. "Are they loving people?"

With a sigh, she gazed at him and shrugged. "I guess my mother was when I was little, but the nanny took care of me and my sister."

He couldn't imagine another person taking care of the children in the family besides the mother. "You had a nanny? What exactly did she do?"

Bella must have come from a wealthy family to have had a nanny. Why did she need the bakery then? What was she not being honest about?

"Oh, Beatrice was very good to us. She arranged our clothing. Took us to the park, and if we had a birthday party we attended, she took us."

"When did you see your mother?"

Bella smiled. "Every morning she came in and had tea with us and talked to us about what we were going to do that day. Then at night, she would come up and kiss us goodnight. If we saw her in the house during the day, we could go into her parlor if she didn't have guests. But mother was very active in society. Often times, we wouldn't see her for days because she was planning or hosting a big party."

Luca thought of his own mother and how she had been there at his side right up until the day she'd died. He couldn't imagine anything being more important than your children. No parties, no teas, not a single social event.

"Where does your family live?"

She glanced at him, her brown eyes, shadowed with anxiety and then glanced out at the gently babbling river. "Boston."

"I know you're friends with Miss Vanderhooten. Is that how you came to be here in New Hope? You're so far from the people who love you, and I couldn't imagine my brother or sister moving so far away. Don't you want to go home?"

A sarcastic laugh escaped her lips. "Yes, I came out because of Abigail, but no, I don't want to go home. You're a man. You don't know what it's like to be a woman. You're a commodity to be sold at auction to the highest bidder who has the right credentials. I want to live my life the way I think is best, not the way my father wants."

Luca thought about his own father and how they argued over the bakery, but he was a man. And he would not let his father, as much as he loved him, decide the fate of his life. He understood and admired how Bella stood up and protected her right to choose. But moving away from the people you love. He knew he would never leave his family. His roots were here.

"So will you return to Boston?"

"Someday, but not now. Not anytime soon," she said. "Let's eat. I'm starving."

She seemed to completely shut down the discussion on her family and returning to Boston. Something wasn't right. He didn't know what, but it almost felt like she was hiding something.

They pulled out the Caprese salad Cara created along with one of Bella's loaves of bread with baked cheese on the slices.

"It's not much," Luca said, laying out the glass plates for them to eat on.

"It's fabulous," Bella said. "Look what she did with the bread. I love that. And the fresh tomatoes and cheese and basil."

"Cara likes to make her own cheese, so I can promise this will be very good."

He pulled out the bottle of wine and pulled the cork out. "From my vineyard."

He handed her a glass and she waited until he'd poured his own. Clinking their goblets together, he said, "Enjoy, or as Italians say, godere."

"Godere," she repeated and then sipped the red wine. "Very good."

"You like it?"

"Very much. I'm not normally a red wine person, but this has such a sweet flavor to it."

"I'm so glad you like it. It's one of the first bottles from last year's grapes."

"I didn't know you had a vineyard."

"I started it the year Mama died. I needed something to occupy my mind. I found it hard to go into the bakery after she was gone. I felt her presence everywhere I looked and my grief almost overwhelmed me."

Closing his eyes, pain rushed over him once again. His mother's smiling face and how she loved him so much. Death had stolen his mother from the family way before her time and his heart still ached with the loss. "She had been telling me I should start a vineyard and make wine. So I did. I tilled the soil, bought some grapes, and I've been working at it since then.

"I hope someday it will replace the money we lost when we decided to close the bakery. I need the cash from the sale of the bakery to put in more grapes, build a wine cellar, bottles, and wine barrels. That's the reason I want to sell the bakery. Not to make your life more difficult."

Talking to Bella was so easy and he hadn't meant to confess his reasons for needing to sell the store, it had just come out. But now she knew why he needed the money. Maybe now she would understand why she couldn't continue at the bakery after the six weeks were up.

She looked down. "I didn't know. But if I paid you rent, wouldn't that help you."

He shook his head. He'd ran the numbers and he needed a lot more than what she was offering a month to purchase the supplies. "Not really. But we promised we weren't going to talk about the bakery, and here we are, talking about the one thing that upsets both of us."

"You're right. We should just enjoy today." Bella crunched into a bite of the cheesy bread and licked her lips. "This is so nice, Luca. Sitting outside in the sunshine, drinking wine, and eating cheesy bread with you. I'm really enjoying myself."

He smiled, happy to hear exactly what he was feeling. While he reminded himself he was only doing this to distract her from her business, it didn't feel that way. It felt better. Like this was how they were meant to spend the afternoon.

They ate the salad and the cheese and bread and finally Bella pushed her plate away. "Enough. I can't eat anymore."

"But wait, I brought grapes from the vineyard."

He plucked a few and popped them into her mouth. She smiled at him as she chewed the grapes. "Sweet and delicious."

Her sweet mouth was just too tempting. He leaned down and pressed his lips against hers. He could taste the grapes on her lips, the sweetness intensifying with the taste of Bella.

Why did he enjoy kissing her so much? Why this woman who frustrated, bedeviled him and tempted him more than any woman he'd ever met. Pressing against her mouth, he could feel her falling and he fell with her down to the blanket, covering the top half of her body, crushing her breasts against his chest. His mouth moved over her warm and supple lips pummeling her tender mouth, his blood pounding through his veins. He needed her closer, he needed her beneath him, begging him to take her and if she said yes, he would have her in a heartbeat.

Her arms wound around his neck, pulling him closer and he wished they were naked, skin to skin. He released her lips, whispering Italian words calling her beautiful, telling her how much he wanted her, thankful she couldn't understand the language. Her hand caressed the side of his face, running up through his hair as she moaned beneath him. He trailed his fingers down her neck, down her shoulder, and across her chest.

Tenderly he let his fingers trail across the mounds of her breasts and she arched, pressing against his hand. He kissed down her neck and across her chest until his mouth was just above the décolleté of her dress. He kissed the spot tenderly and she moaned, the sound deep in her throat as she held his head in place.

It was then he felt the first few raindrops splattering across his face, her chest. He glanced up at the sky and noticed the gathering of storm clouds. Why couldn't have the rain held off a little longer, just a few more hours in her arms? "The sky is about to open on us, mio caro."

She rose to a sitting position, forcing him from her breasts. "We should go."

He kissed her softly on the lips. "But I was enjoying our time together."

"Me too," she said softly.

Just then the skies opened and quickly they jumped up, throwing the leftover food in the basket. With the blanket over their heads, they looked at each other and laughed.

"Oh, Bella," he said. "You're going to make my life difficult."

His lips lowered onto hers again as he kissed her in the rain.

~

Bella sat staring out the window of the bakery. She'd come home from her picnic with Luca and immediately gone down and made eight loaves of bread. Now while the bread was baking, she sat with pen and paper and again contemplated what she was doing.

Today, Luca had shared his dream of the vineyard and how it would help his family replace the money they'd lost when they closed the bakery. He needed the money from the sale of the bakery to buy equipment for his dream. And with her leasing the bakery, his own dream was on hold. He was sacrificing for her and that just didn't feel right.

His father and sister had been so kind to her, and she saw the love the four of them had for one another and wished her family had the same closeness.

Her father was probably searching for her, but she wasn't going to live by his threats any longer. If he disinherited her that was fine, but she needed to face them and tell him no more future husbands being paraded in front of her. No more telling her to come home to Boston. She was an independent woman and she was done with running.

It was time she confronted her father and told him she also wanted access to the money in her account. She would take that money and purchase the bakery from Luca, so he could live his dream. She was currently living hers and she didn't want to be the person who kept him from acquiring his dream.

She had no idea where this thing between the two of them was headed, but she knew that whatever it was, it felt right. When she was with him, it seemed like she'd come home to where she belonged and who she was meant to spend her life with. And for that reason, she needed to warn her father and let him know she would not accept any more of his schemes to get her to marry. She was done.

Picking up the pen, she glanced down at the paper, sighed, and finally had the words exactly like she wanted them.

In New Hope, Texas. Need money. Don't come if you expect me to marry someone you choose. I've already found someone.

She knew telegram operators were notorious gossips and knew everyone in town, but she wanted her family to know she wasn't going to marry someone her father had chosen. The image of Luca with raindrops splattering his face as he kissed her had her heart leaping into her throat. She didn't know where they were headed, but she liked the direction they were going. And now, maybe she could help him achieve his dream.

After she took the bread out of the oven, she walked down the street to the telegraph office. She was taking a huge risk in letting everyone know where she was, but it was time to stop hiding and face them. She was after all, an educated woman, a suffragette, and she was fearless. Or at least, she liked to believe she was strong.

Chapter Seven

A week later, Bella was waiting outside the church for Luca to appear. He'd told her he had a surprise for her. The wind gusted, blowing hot dust rippling down the street. Fall was here.

At home, the leaves would have already started turning, but here in Texas, the heat lingered. Though the nights had finally started to cool off, she kept waiting for the first sign of fall and hopefully soon, winter. But right now, she was sweating, it was so warm.

Finally, she saw him driving up to the church. He pulled the wagon to a halt and then jumped down. "Sorry, I'm late, but the priest was there today and the mass was long."

"There's not a priest there every Sunday?"

"No, only twice a month. He travels, visiting other church's in the area," he said helping her up into the wagon.

"What are we doing today?" she asked sitting on the bench.

Maybe today she would tell him the truth about her real name and her father searching for her and how he could be showing up any day. Maybe today, he would learn she was really a shipping heiress and wealthy beyond his wildest dreams.

He climbed onto the wagon, turned to her, and smiled. "Papa would like for you to come to an early dinner tonight. He said he knows that you must work in the bakery this evening, but he'd like for you to see our home."

"I'd love to," she said with a smile. "But that's later this afternoon. What are we going to do?"

Luca grinned and she couldn't help but wonder what he was up to. He took her hand, raised it to his lips and kissed the back of her hand. "Oh, how I've missed you this week. We'll find something to keep us busy."

She knew exactly what she wanted to do with Luca and it involved lots of kissing. She leaned her head against his shoulder. Why was it this man seemed to warm all the places in her heart and fill her with such joy? "Did you have a good week?"

"Yes. How about you? Did the bakery do well?"

They had agreed not to talk about the bakery, but how could she not tell him they had broken all the records they set and it was their best week ever. She was starting to have returning clients and that made her feel so good. To know people were coming back to experience more of her baking.

"It went very well," was all she said, keeping the numbers close to her heart. Right now her life couldn't be better, except for the fact she knew her dream was keeping Luca from completing his dreams. "How is the vineyard?"

"We begin picking the grapes next week. So I will be very busy," he said. "This year, I'm making even more wine."

If the bakery continued to do well, she would soon be able to show him how she would repay him. She wanted to be the one to give him what he needed to achieve his dream.

She smiled. "Will you need help? I'm sure the girls wouldn't mind picking grapes if you paid them a little something to help with their expenses," she said.

He glanced at her and his lips turned up. "I may just take you up on that offer. I don't want Papa out there, especially in this heat. It seems the summer will never end."

The leaves on the trees were still green with no sign of them beginning to turn. While she missed St. Louis, she didn't know if she would ever return to Boston. There was nothing there to draw her back.

"Yes, it has been extremely warm. In Boston, the leaves would already be colorful. This is my favorite time of year there."

"Don't expect the leaves to change here until early November."

"That's surprising," she responded.

"Yes, sometimes we go straight from summer to winter, without a fall in between."

Occasionally, his thigh would touch her leg and warmth would fill her, rushing through her veins and straight to her heart. No matter what happened with the bakery, she couldn't help but think she was beginning to have real feelings for Luca and that both thrilled and frightened her.

She'd never really been in love before. There had been boys who'd kissed her, but no man had made her hunger for him the way Luca's kisses seared her.

The wagon rolled along and soon they were out of town. "When are you going to let me know where we're going?"

He was being almost secretive about what he had planned for today and that made her even more curious.

"First, I thought we would go by the vineyard and I'd show you my grapes."

"I can't wait," she said excitedly. This was his dream and she wanted to share it with him.

The wagon pulled up in front of a field of grapevines. "These are the first vines I planted, the year Mama died. They are two years old, so they're maturing. The best grapes come from these vines."

She could hear the pride in his voice and ached.

"Where did you learn so much about grapes?"

"My great-grandfather had a vineyard in Italy. Mama knew quite a bit about vineyards and kept telling me I was the one who should start a vineyard here."

He jumped down from the wagon and then reached up to help her alight. She felt his hands on her waist and her heart beat increased as she stared down into his dark eyes. She longed to caress the side of his face but thought that would be acting forward. When her feet touched the ground, he released her. "Over that ridge, there, is our house."

"You're not as far from town as I feared."

"No, in fact, Papa would have liked to have been further out, but Mama insisted we stay close to the bakery. It's a good thing," Luca said.

Grabbing the quilt from the back of the wagon, he turned to her and grabbed her hand. They walked to the edge of the field of vines and she saw the grapes ripening on the stems.

"You want to wait until the grapes are at their ripest before you pick them. This way they will have the highest concentrate of sugar."

"So how do you decide when to pick them?"

He smiled and wiped the sweat from his brow. "Go ahead, pick one and eat it."

She plucked the grape from the vine. She let the taste roll around on her tongue. "It's ripe, but it could be riper."

"Yes," he said. "The only way to know when to pick the grapes is when your tongue tells you it's time. And then you need to pick them as soon as possible."

The field was full of stalks with vines loaded with fresh grapes. She glanced at Luca as he walked amongst the vines, checking them carefully, so proud of his work.

Walking towards her, she felt her heart beating rapidly in her chest at the sight of this strong, viral man who made her hotter than the summer heat. "Where will you plant your new vines?"

"You can't see it from here, but we own the land on the other side of this field. I soon hope to have all our fields covered with vines. Then we will be the largest producer in Texas."

Sensing his excitement, she couldn't help but feel guilty she was what was standing in his way.

He reached down and brushed the hair from her face, his fingers caressing her cheek. "Walk with me. I will show you my second favorite spot."

They strolled along the grapevines and occasionally he would pluck a grape and pop it into his mouth. "Not yet."

She heard the sound of the river before she saw the water. When they left the vineyard, they walked through a grove of trees and there before them was a cool, inviting clear water creek. The water babbled over rocks, enticing and rambling before it went into a wide river.

Bella was hot, she was thirsty, and now the sight of the cool water made her want to groan. The heat was miserable today.

Spreading the quilt under a shade tree, he dropped her hand and pulled his shirt over his head.

Her mouth open at the sight of his bare chest, his muscles carved like stone across his stomach. The man was a god and she wanted to reach out and touch his bare flesh but knew that would not be appropriate. He glanced at her and grinned. "It's hot. I'm going for a dip. Come with me?"

Licking her lips nervously she glanced around and then to her astonishment he dropped his pants. Standing before her in his long johns, his muscles clearly outlined. His manhood prominent in the clinging cloth.

"Luca?" she gasped amazed at the forwardness of the man.

"What? It's hot. We're broiling out here. I'm going to cool off."

"You could swim in your clothes," she said.

He grinned at her. "I'm a man. I'm not ashamed of my body and you shouldn't be either."

Staring at him she felt stunned. What should she do? She couldn't very well leave and she didn't want to. If she were honest with herself, she was falling in love with Luca. Her heart, her body, her very soul longed to join him in that cool stream.

"You can keep your underclothes on," he said as he ran to the river's edge and leaped into the water much like a boy.

The splashing sounds were too much as he disappeared beneath the water. When he came up, he wiped the water from his face. "Come on in. It will cool you off."

Oh my, she wanted to so badly, but it wasn't proper. She could ruin her reputation if anyone found out. Sweat poured down her back, leaving her dress clinging to her.

But it would feel so good.

She was a suffragette. She was an independent, forward thinking woman. She could jump in the water if she wanted to. Turning her back to him, she unbuttoned her dress and pulled it from her hot body. The cool breeze touched her skin and she felt so much relief.

Quickly she pulled off her shoes and socks and wound her hair up high on top of her head and shoved the pins to keep it in place. Dressed in only her chemise and pantaloons she crept to the edge.

The water lapped at her toes, feeling almost cold. The coolness was all the temptation she needed.

Luca rose out of the river like a Greek god, his body shimmering with water. He held out his hand and she took it to keep from slipping on the rocks. He led her into the center of the river where the water was cool and she sank up to her neck. "Oh my goodness, this feels wonderful."

He smiled and pulled her into his wet arms. They bobbed in the water, his eyes dark with a fire she could feel in her own blood. "You are beautiful. A wet river nymph."

Feeling self-conscious at her near naked state, she laid her hands on his bare skin. Heat sizzled through her and it wasn't from the sun. This was a heat only Luca created within her. She ran her fingers down his chest and watched as his eyes widened and his nose flared. He cursed.

"Am I hurting you?" she asked.

"No, you fill me with hunger," he said softly in her ear. "I want you like a man wants a woman."

He stepped in between her legs and she could feel his erection hard against her center.

"Oh," she said with surprise.

He smiled at her. "You make me hard for you."

His words made her heart beat fast as she lifted her hands to his face and pulled his mouth down to hers. She wanted him just as much as he desired her. And even if this wasn't meant to be forever, she hungered to show Luca her love. For she knew that even with the issues of the bakery facing them, she'd fallen in love with him. It was why she had decided to contact her family and expected her father to arrive any day. But before he got here, she longed to make certain she was Luca's woman. No one else's.

His lips moved over hers, possessing her with a hunger she'd never experienced before. He pressed his rigid, hard member between her legs and she knew her decision was made. No matter what happened tomorrow, today she was Luca's woman.

Finally, she pulled back from him. "I've never done this before, but I want you, Luca. I want to experience what happens between a man and a woman with you."

"Madre Dios," he said beneath his breath and covered her mouth with his.

~

Luca pulled Bella out of the water and moved her to the blanket he'd spread on the ground. Her chemise and pantaloons were plastered to her skin, the shadow of her nipples showed through the wet material and he lowered his mouth and sucked the tender orb into his mouth. She gasped and tilted her head back giving him more access.

"Oh, mio caro," he whispered against her breast. "You are beauty and fire."

She moved into his arms, and her mouth lifted in eager anticipation of his sensual assault, surrender only a heartbeat away.

Luca poured his soul into his kiss, and all the pent-up desire he'd kept dammed came flooding out. A moan resounded from his throat as his lips sought and plundered hers. He felt like a drowning man going down for the final time as he pulled her close, her wet breasts crushed against his chest.

Why did this woman affect him like none before her? How was it she had managed to get under his skin when none of the others had? He craved her touch like a man addicted to opium and didn't care that she was the reason his own dreams were on hold. He needed her like the earth needed rain.

She tasted of honey and sweetness, of passion and tangled sheets, and he wanted nothing more than to take her to bed and slip into her womanly sheath, but they were outside under the trees, next to a babbling stream.

Mindless sex would not suffice with this woman. He wanted her body and soul, her eager and willing. He wanted her like no other woman before. Only Bella seemed to fill the emptiness inside him that sent him into the vineyard.

He wrenched his lips away from hers, his breathing hard and fast. "Are you certain this is what you want?"

"Kiss me again before I change my mind."

                  Sylvia McDaniel

Luca needed no further invitation. His lips eagerly sought hers as he pulled her onto the quilt beside him. She gave a soft sigh of pleasure, her eyes half closed.

"Is this wrong?" she whispered.

"No, not between us. This has been building for so long."

She turned to face him, her hand reaching out tentatively to caress his cheek. "I want you."

"Oh, mio caro," he said under his breath thinking that no woman had ever told him that she wanted him. Never before, and he felt like this was where he belonged. She was his home, his hearth, and his world. He wanted her even more than she desired him.

His lips closed over hers, seeking to lose himself in her body. He sought the edges of her mouth, gently nipping her with his teeth until she opened for him. Like a starved man, his tongue swept the inside of her mouth, plundering and receiving pleasure beyond his dreams. She returned his kiss with an equal passion of her own, stunning him with the intensity.

His hand reached down and tugged on her chemise. Finally, she broke from his kiss and reached between them and pulled the garment over her head. Her breasts were small, sweet melons that he eagerly placed his mouth on, tasting and squeezing them. "Your skin is like silk and your breasts are beautiful."

Eagerly he suckled her hardened nipple. She moaned a low, throaty noise as he untied the drawstring on her pantaloons and pushed them down.

Sunlight glistened on her wet skin and he sucked in his breath at the sight of her naked flesh. She was more than he'd ever imagined. Her body must have been crafted by the angels to leave a man aching with desire. Her tiny waist and rounded hips, her skin was white and soft as a newborn babe, her areolas a strawberry pink.

His hand sought and caressed her womanly apex. The honey of her arousal was warm against his fingers. She arched upward against his hand, seeking fulfillment. His Bella was so responsive to his touch, and he couldn't help but be eager to get inside her body.

Quickly, he shed his long johns and slid next to Bella's satin skin. He was strength and hardness; she was softness and silk.

They lay side by side, her breath a soft caress against his lips. He drank in the sight of her body next to his and felt intoxicated with desire. Taking her hand, he moved it down his body until her fingers rested on the stem of his passion.

Her fingertips ran over his maleness, touching the tip gingerly. He reached for the center of her as his fingers delved into her while she stroked him.

For every caress he gave Bella, she returned one, until Luca felt as if he were ablaze. Every time she touched him, the heat of his need flamed anew until he wasn't sure who consumed whom.

Finally, unable to stand the heat any longer, he rose above her on the quilt and urged her legs apart. Slowly he pressed into her womanly sheath, into her welcome heat, meeting the resistance of her maidenhead.

Knowing he was taking her virginity, he stared down at this tiny woman who had completely changed his world. Caro Dio in cielo, he loved this woman. Sometime over the last few weeks, he'd fallen in love with her.

Her hands clutched his back as he thrust into her, and she held onto him, giving as much as she received. Never before had he been given so much pleasure from a woman. Never before had his heart reacted to a woman's soft cries of passion. Never before had he seen such innocence and sweetness in a woman. His woman. His Bella.

Using every ounce of willpower he commanded, he was gentle and caring. With every ounce of strength, he withheld his own pleasure until he thought he would explode.

She was heaven and she was hell. Heaven in that he wanted this to last forever, hell because he knew that with each stroke he came closer to release. Came closer to losing control of both his body and his soul.

With a gasp of astonishment, she dug her nails into his back, clinging to him as she cried out his name. That was all Luca needed to send him over the edge. The sound of her crying out in pleasure sent him spiraling over the top, spilling his seed deep within her.

He collapsed, his mind whirling in a thousand directions. She had been tentative and shy with her caresses, but he had made her his in every sense of the word.

~

Bella's heart was overflowing with love. After they made love, they'd gone swimming naked in the river, kissing and loving on one another. Too quickly the sun had started to descend, cooling their overheated bodies. They knew it was time to go to dinner, but the afternoon had been magical. One Bella would never forget. They had dried each other off with the blanket and then dressed.

"I'm anxious to have dinner with your family," she said as the wagon pulled up in front of the house.

"Why?" he said turning to glance at her.

"I'm afraid they will see on my face the glow you've put in my cheeks and know how we spent the afternoon."

He smiled and caressed her face with his fingers. "Oh, Bella, there is a glow, but I think your skin was kissed by the sun today."

"And you," she said blushing.

He kissed the tip of her nose. "Come, we're already late."

He helped her from the wagon and then they hurried into the house.

"Ciao," he called as they walked through the door.

The house was a rustic farmhouse, but Bella could tell it was filled with love. They walked into a large room, a horsehair couch and a couple of rocking chairs centered around the fireplace. A table already set for dinner was in the corner close to an open doorway that Bella felt certain led to the kitchen.

It was not a large house, but it looked comfortable and homey. She thought of the mansion her parents lived in and realized their home had never had this feeling of warmth and family.

Cara stepped from the kitchen. "There you are. We were starting to get worried."

"Yes, I was showing her the vines and it took longer than I thought," Luca said, smiling warmly at Bella.

"Can I help you?" she said to Cara.

"Oh no, Papa has been helping me and we're just about ready." She grinned at her brother "You have a leaf in your hair," she said quietly and went back into the kitchen.

Bella's cheeks burned and she felt mortified as she watched Luca reach up and run his hands through his hair, shaking out the leaf that was entangled.

"I didn't see it," Bella whispered.

He laughed. "Oh, well. It could have blown in there."

Franco came out carrying a roasted chicken. "Ciao, Bella. I hope you're hungry."

She was starving. "Ciao, Franco, and I can't wait to eat. That smells delicious."

After the afternoon of swimming and lovemaking, she felt hungry and tired and she didn't want this day to end.

He grinned. "Sit. You will sit beside Luca."

"Ricci," Cara called. "Time to eat."

The youngest of the clan came bounding down the stairs. He was a much younger version of Luca and she smiled at the sight of him. "Hello."

"Hello," he said smiling at her. "You must be Bella."

"Yes, nice to meet you."

He nodded and then they all sat.

Franco said the evening prayer and then they began to pass the plate of chicken and salad. "What did you think of the vineyard."

"I think Luca is going to have a lot of work to do in the next few weeks."

His father smiled at him. "He's going to have the best wine in the country. People in town can enjoy a true Italian experience. Good bread, fine wine, and someday Cara will sell her wonderful cheese."

"Oh, Papa. You are biased," Cara said with a smile.

"No, it's good cheese," Bella said. "I enjoyed it very much at lunch today."

Cara gazed at the two of them. "I think you two look absolutely glowing. Is there something you need to tell us?"

Luca grinned at his sister and then his father, but didn't say anything.

"You know Papa has said all along that Bella was the girl for you. So he told you not to bother or distract her because she needed to focus on the bakery. I don't think you took his advice."

Luca laughed. "I took his advice. I've been doing my best to distract Bella."

A cold chill wound its way up Bella's spine. The time they had been spending together was not just to pull her away from the bakery was it?

Franco frowned and glanced at Bella. "We all want Bella to be successful with the bakery. That's why I said don't disturb her."

Tense Bella glanced at Luca. She could see he was starting to fiddle with this food like he felt uncomfortable.

"We have agreed not to talk about the bakery until the time when we determine when she's been successful or not," he said.

"Well, it appears that the two of you are spending a lot of time away from the bakery together," Cara said.

Franco was frowning. "I told you to stay away from Bella, because I thought she needed time to learn the business, to build up her clientele. I would be happy if she was my daughter-in-law, but not until you decide the status of the bakery."

Bella was growing more and more bitter. Was Luca only spending time with her to get her focus off her dream? If so, she had fallen right into his hands, and in the process, she'd given him her heart.

"The status of the bakery is unchanged. I am selling it just as soon as her six weeks are up," he said not looking at her.

No matter how hard she worked or what she did, he was going to reach his goal and leave her searching for some new place to bake. Even if she could buy the bakery from him, she suddenly doubted he would sell it to her.

Suddenly everything she'd thought they had together seemed a lie. She'd fallen in love with a man who didn't want to see her succeed, but fail so his dream would be a great success.

The rest of the meal was a tense silence.

Luca was frowning at his sister and father, and Bella didn't say a word, her heart quietly breaking.

When they were finished, she turned to Luca. "It's getting late. You should take me back to town. I need to get back to the bakery."

He nodded as Cara began to clear the table.

"Thank you for the lovely dinner. It was delicious," she said as she walked toward the door.

She just wanted to escape, to get away from the tension in the room. She also wanted to talk to Luca. Had he been doing what his sister hinted at? Trying to court her away from the bakery and guarantee its demise?

Walking to the door, Franco came up behind her. "I will see you tomorrow, Bella."

"Yes, thanks for the dinner," she said and walked out the door. Why did she have the feeling that somehow his family had just ratted on Luca? And why was her heart hurting so badly at that thought? She knew she was in love with Luca, she'd given him her heart, but if he was trying to end her dreams, it would devastate her.

~

Luca glanced at Bella as they rode along in the buggy. She'd been quiet since they left the house, sitting rigidly beside him on the wagon, staring straight ahead. He hadn't been around that many women in his life, but he knew enough to know she must be angry.

"Do you want to talk about it?"

"Talk about what?" she asked.

"About why you're so upset."

"I'm trying to decide if I have a reason to be mad at you. Is it true?"

Luca was not going to admit to anything. "I don't understand why you're irritated. What do you think I've done?"

She turned on the seat and glared at him in the darkness, but he looked straight ahead.

He loved this woman and had planned on confessing his love to her tonight, but not if they were going to fight. And yet a part of him felt guilty. He had gone to the bakery to distract her. He knew for a fact, but instead she had gained his heart. If only his sister had kept her mouth shut, everything would have been just fine.

"Did you intend to distract me from my business? Is that why you've been coming to the bakery and kissing me and..." She looked away and he saw her swipe a tear from her eye.

He pulled the wagon up in front of the bakery and wrapped the reins around the brake handle with every intention of pulling her into his arms. He turned toward her and she scooted away from him. "Answer my question."

He bit down on his lip, not wanting to be honest with her, wishing he could lie, but knowing it was better to tell her the truth, even if it made her mad.

"Yes, originally I came hoping to keep you from making the bakery a success. But then, I kissed you and I haven't been able to stop thinking of you since the day we both had flour all over us. And after today, I..."

Why did it sound so feeble? Like he wasn't sincere. Like he'd just lied to her to steal her dream.

"You know the bakery is my dream. It means as much to me as your vineyard means to you. I love the baking and I want to be an independent woman who didn't need to marry a man for her wellbeing. After being at the vineyard, I thought you of all people would understand," she said softly. "And then tonight, I find you're just spending time with me to keep me from being a success, so you can have your dream."

"No, no, no. I have said all along I wanted to see you be a success."

Why did he feel like this was getting worse by the second?

"Just not my bakery. And how can I be a success without someplace to sell my goods?"

He licked his lips, knowing he'd done wrong and regretting his focus on trying to keep her from the bakery. Yet, it was the only way his vineyard would get the funding it needed.

"That's like saying I want your wine to be successful, but I hope your grapes aren't sweet," she said, shaking her head. "I thought we had something I've never felt before, but maybe not."

What had he done that was so awful? He'd not done anything to disparage her. He'd not harmed the bakery. He'd kissed her and taken her on several picnics and realized he was the biggest damn fool for even thinking of getting her away from her dream.

"Bella, I didn't do anything. It's not like I damaged the flour or yeast or even told people not to show up. I began our courtship with the idea of pulling you away from the bakery."

"And once I failed at the bakery, what were you going to do?" she asked looking into his dark eyes.

What could he say? He had thought that would be the end of it. They would never see each other again and he would walk away.

She would be sad the bakery closed and their courtship was over and he would go away unscathed. But he wasn't unscathed. He was frightened now that he was about to lose her and he didn't know how to answer her question without appearing cold and calculating, which he was realizing too late, he was.

She sighed. "You obviously don't want to answer that question." She held onto the wagon, swung her leg over and started climbing down. Quickly he jumped from the wagon, racing to her side, but by the time he got there, her feet were on the ground.

She gazed at him. "Today was magical, right up until your sister enlightened me, and I learned the truth. This is not going to work. I have indeed let you distract me. Give me the rest of my time at the bakery to find a new building and then we'll move out."

"No, Bella, I don't want us to end."

She turned and gazed sadly at him. "You should have thought about that when you decided to try to ruin my business. To end my dream."

She hurried into the bakery, opening and closing the door. Locking it behind her.

Luca stood in the street, gazing at the lighted windows as she made her way to the back of the building. Blowing out the lantern, he felt like she'd just extinguished the fire in his soul. He was the stupidest man alive in the state of Texas.

Chapter Eight

The next morning, Bella walked down into the bakery she had come to love. There was a quiet peacefulness about the shop this time of day she enjoyed puttering around in. This was when she tried new recipes. Tried to better old ones or just sat with a cup of coffee, watching the sun rise to the smell of freshly baking bread. The business was finally starting to make a profit, she was seeing repeat customers and now she had to start from scratch once again.

Callie came down the stairs. "There you are. Are you okay?"

"I'm fine," she said, though inside her heart was breaking. She loved Luca. Had given herself to him body and soul only to learn he was more interested in making certain the bakery failed than in her.

"Frankly, I think we should bake him a nice delicious prune pie. Fill it with enough castor oil that he would spend a lot of time either in the vineyard or in the outhouse."

This is what she loved about her friends. Last night they rallied around her, supporting her when the tears had fallen and she'd told them the truth. That no matter what they did, Luca would sell the bakery out from under them to obtain his dream.

Bella smiled. "I wish I could, but I can't do that to him. His father has been so kind to me. I should feel thankful that his sister accidentally revealed his true nature."

"You really think it was accidental?"

"Yes, I do because Franco was most unhappy and so was Luca."

The quietness of the table and the pained expressions on Luca's and Franco's face last night made her believe that Cara had unwittingly said something she shouldn't.

And thank God she had, or Bella would have been crushed when he told her to move out of the bakery.

"Do you think Franco was in on this?" Callie questioned.

"I don't think so."

Bella took a sip of coffee. "So now I need to start looking for us a new place to live and a new place to create a bakery. Or maybe I should just go home."

The thought of going to St. Louis wasn't as awful as it sounded yesterday. Maybe there, she could start a bakery. But then again, there her father would be furious she had a business and doing menial labor. She doubted he would ever understand that she baked because she loved the smell of yeast and the different aromas drifting out of the oven.

Callie shook her head. "Think long and hard before you decide to go home. You know we love you and want you here with us. But if you think you should go, I understand. When things get tough, it's hard being away from the ones we love."

"Ha, I get more love from you girls and Lu..." she trailed off. She couldn't use the two words in the same sentence and say them out loud because then everyone would realize she had fallen in love with the man. She would keep those words closely guarded.

She sighed. "We'll see. I haven't made my decision just yet. But the bakery is gone. I now realize we don't have a chance of keeping it."

"You look tired. Why don't you let me and Diamond cover the front today."

She thought about it for a moment. Then stopped to watch the sun rise, its rays lighting the sky. It was a new day. A new beginning. And she would rise up once again, just like she always did.

She'd given herself completely to Luca, but she was an independent woman. She would be fine. Only now, she feared her father was on his way and how could she convince him she wanted to stay here. And did she really want to?

"I think I will spend some time in the kitchen baking today. It always seems to soothe my soul when I have flour between my fingers."

Callie smiled. "We'll take care of the store."

"I'm going to run to the bank. Maybe you should go with me since you want to open an account here in town."

"Yes, I'll go with you and we can visit the bank together."

"Thanks. I don't know what I'd do if I didn't have all of you," she whispered feeling tears welling in her eyes.

She hadn't told them what had happened between her and Luca for fear they would have hunted him down. But she knew in her heart and would carry that afternoon by the river with her forever.

~

As the sun rose, Luca rode into town, bleary-eyed after spending most of the night thinking he'd just made the biggest mistake of his life. The image of her face while in the throes of passion would sneak up on him and then he'd remember how he'd broken her heart. He had to speak with her before his father arrived at the bakery this morning.

He strode through the door of the store just as they were opening. A woman he'd never seen before stood behind the counter. "Where's Bella?"

She smiled at him. "What would you like, sir? We have fresh bread, shortbread cookies, apple turnovers, or cream pastry."

"I want to see Bella," he said anger rising in him filling him.

"I'm sorry, but she's concentrating on her business and we're not allowed to interrupt her," the redhead said.

"Seems someone tried to use her to his advantage, and now she's more determined than ever to make the bakery a success."

Luca took a deep breath knowing if he released the fury that flowed from him, it would get him nowhere. Another woman came to the counter. "Is there a problem, Diamond?"

"No problem, just a hound dog looking for a bone."

"Look, I know you probably think the worst of me, and I don't care, but I need to speak to Bella. I want to make things right between us," he said.

The woman named Diamond stared at him. "She doesn't want to see you."

His chest felt like someone had punched him. If only he could explain what a fool he'd been and how she had changed his life and his mind and he would give her the damn bakery if she'd just speak to him.

"Bella," he yelled. "Bella come out here, right now. I need to talk to you."

The two women looked at each other and then they marched around the counter. One had a broom in her hand and the other a mop. They came on either side of him and grabbed him by the arms and started to pull him towards the door.

"I'm not leaving until I see Bella," he yelled. "Bella."

He dug his heels in refusing to leave. Diamond picked up her broom and hit him on the buttocks. "Leave or I'll get the sheriff."

Just then his father walked in the door. "Luca?"

Luca was a man who would do whatever it took to see his woman.

"They refuse to let me see Bella," he said. "I need to talk to her."

Franco glanced at the women and then at Luca. "Release him. I will take care of him."

His father took him by the arm and led him outside the bakery. "Papa, she won't speak to me. On the drive home last night, she told me we were done. She's mad and believes I didn't want her to be successful and seeing her only to make her fail."

"Were you?" his father asked.

Luca threw his hands into the air. "It started that way, but, Papa, after our first kiss, I fell in love with her. She's my anima gemelli, my soul mate."

At this moment, the bakery, the vineyard, none of it mattered. All that mattered was him getting to speak to Bella.

His father sighed. "When you love someone, Luca, you put their needs above your own. You give them whatever they need to be happy. You get joy in making them contented. And you learn very quickly that when you make a strong woman angry, your life is going to be hell."

"But, Papa, how do I get her back?"

He wanted Bella back. He wanted her in his arms. He wanted to marry her and make her his wife.

"You can't, right now. Walk away and let time work its magic. It may be that you can never repair the damage you've done, but for now, you have to wait until she's ready to hear you."

Luca hung his head. "Papa, is this how you felt about Mama?"

His father laughed. "Yes. And your mother had me ready to jump off the nearest cliff because she refused to speak to me. And then I married her."

Luca looked in the window of the bakery where the two women were almost guarding the door.

"Let me see if I can talk to Bella. You should go to work," he said patting his son on the back. "Let me see what I can do."

Luca gave one last look at the bakery. Why did he feel like he was losing everything? All because he'd gotten greedy and wanted the money from the sale of the bakery to help his vineyard. He'd acted so stupid, and now, he was paying for his lack of good judgement.

~

Bella and Callie sat in front of Samuel O'Brien, the banker at the New Hope Bank and Trust. They had waited almost an hour before he'd finally agreed to see them.

"What can I do for you ladies," he said.

Callie looked at Bella. "I need to open an account."

He leaned back and crossed his arms across his chest. "Are you married?"

"No," she said.

Bella felt a trickle of alarm go down her spine. Wasn't this man Tim Barton's good friend?

"I'm sorry, but per bank policy, we do not open accounts for single women. When you marry, your husband will be free to open an account with us."

"You don't think I have need of a bank account before then?" Callie asked.

He laughed. "Your father or brother, they can take care of any money needs you may have."

Callie laughed and shook her head. "Unbelievable."

"And you, Miss Sullivan, how can I help you?"

"I want to borrow money to purchase the building the bakery is located in."

The man leaned back and laughed out loud. "Bank policy does not allow us to lend money to women."

"Not even a business loan?"

"No, ma'am. Besides, that building is being bought by Tim Barton. You're not going to buy it because he would never sell to a woman."

Bella felt her insides churn. Not only had Luca lied, but the buyer was none other than the hated Tim Barton who had been so rude to her in her own place of business? The devil take them both. Now she was mad. Fighting mad.

She glanced at Callie who seemed to have steam almost coming out her ears. She watched her friend take a deep breath, pick up her reticule and smile at the banker.

"Sir, I'm sure you're one of those crazy men who think a woman's place is in the home, following ten feet behind her husband, but let me make you aware of something you don't know."

She smiled. "My name is Callie Chesterfield. I'm an heiress. At last count, I was worth over a million dollars. I had planned on putting some of my money into your small bank. But doesn't look like that's going to happen, now."

They rose and walked to the door.

Mr. O'Brien's face was red and he sputtered. "Miss Chesterfield."

She turned around and smiled. "Yes?"

"Let me talk to the board and see what we can do."

She shook her head. "I'm afraid it's too late. You see my friend is going to need a loan and a bank to help her business. I have other friends who need a willing bank to help them out. While sitting here listening to you, I thought to myself, this bank needs some competition."

"No," he said staring as his eyes widened in fright.

"Oh, yes. A bank owned by women for women and anyone else who can't get a loan at your place of business."

"Wait. Let's talk."

She smiled. "Good day, Mr. O'Brien."

They walked out the man's office and into the bank lobby that only had a few men doing business.

"Shake the dust off your feet when we walk out the door. We aren't coming back," Bella said, as they strolled through the door.

~

Later that day, Bella had her hands in flour almost up to her elbows as she kneaded the dough. She'd heard Luca screaming her name, but she refused to see him. She was not going to see him until after her six weeks were up, and she could prove to him how successful she'd made the bakery.

She now knew he would never sell the place to her because Tim Barton was the new buyer. But still, she would have the satisfaction of knowing her business had not been derailed by his courtship.

Callie came into the kitchen. "Franco would like to speak to you."

"Send him back," Bella said hoping he wasn't here to plead his son's case.

A few minutes later, Franco came around the corner putting on an apron. "What are we making today?"

She glanced at him suspiciously. "Cinnamon rolls."

He nodded his head. "I've never made them. What can I do to help you?"

That was a good sign. She wasn't ready to talk about Luca with Franco. After this morning's trip to the bank, she was seething mad. Why did society make it so difficult not to depend on a man?

"While I'm finishing this bread dough and getting it ready to rise, you can take that dough in the bowl and punch it down. Then wait about ten minutes."

"What are cinnamon rolls?"

Bella was finding it difficult to talk. She just wanted to sit in a corner and cry, but she was not going to give Luca the satisfaction of knowing how much he'd hurt her.

"It's a Finnish recipe our cook use to make. They're a pastry with cinnamon and sugar wrapped inside the dough and then on top you put cream icing. When I was a child, it was my favorite pastry. I was kind of missing home today and decided to make some."

"I can't wait to try them," he said punching the dough. "We really enjoyed having you for dinner the other night. Cara is worried she may have caused problems between you and Luca."

She didn't want the girl to feel bad that her comments were what ended their courtship. In fact, Bella felt grateful the girl had told her what was going on.

"No problems between me and Luca. I now know exactly how things are between us."

Bella's chest ached at the way even saying his name brought up so many emotions. She'd trusted him completely. But to sell the bakery to that creepy Tim Barton, that made her angry. If Luca loved the memories he had of his mother and father in the bakery, why would he let this man buy the place?

"In some ways, Luca is like you. He is fixated on being a success. He sometimes does things that if he were older and wiser, he would know was foolish. I have just as big a part to play in this scheme of his, I'm afraid."

Bella felt her heart almost stop. She'd come to trust Franco and his opinions, she liked the old man and now he was telling her he'd also wanted her to fail?

He sighed. "You see, I thought if I baited Luca into seeing you, he would fall in love with you. And you, dear Bella, are exactly the kind of woman I want for my son. I dreamed of the two of you falling in love and marriage and bambinos. So I am just as much to blame as him."

If she had her way, he would never know how much she'd thought the same thing. She'd been dreaming of marriage and babies with Luca, but not anymore.

"But you didn't want me to fail. You've helped me, showing me shortcuts and ways to sell more items. You have been a huge help to me. Luca wanted the bakery not to make a profit so he could sell the building. My dream is not as important as his."

Franco sighed. "I fear you're right. But I had hoped he would see the value of the bakery enough that he would decide to keep them both. I'm not going to interfere, but I hope somehow the two of you will work this out."

Bella closed her eyes and shook her head, her heart breaking. After what she'd learned yesterday, she didn't know if she could forgive Luca.

"I don't see how. I'm going to start looking for a place to have the bakery, and if I can't find one, then I'm returning to St. Louis to my family."

Callie came running into the kitchen, her eyes wide. "Bella. You have to come out to the front."

She gazed at her strangely. "Why?"

"Your father is here."

She felt her heart skip a beat. Could this day get any worse?

Sighing, she turned and looked at Callie. "I'll be right out."

Chapter Nine

Bella went upstairs and freshened up, washing the flour from her hands. Then she asked Callie to send her father upstairs. They needed somewhere to talk privately, away from her customers. As she waited, she glanced around the apartment and wondered what he would think. It wasn't exactly a mansion, but it was nice. Too bad she'd be moving out soon.

She heard the creak on the stairs. She opened the door surprised at the sudden flood of tears that filled her eyes. No matter what, she still loved her father and mother.

"Father," she said blinking rapidly.

He took her in his arms and kissed her on the cheek. "Bella, we've been worried sick. Your mother feared you were dead."

She'd never thought they would think her dead. She had put her parents through a terrible ordeal and for that she was sorry. But she had to find her own way. She knew that more than ever.

"I'm sorry, Father. But when you told me you were coming to Boston to take me home and that you'd found a man for me to marry, I panicked and ran."

She motioned for him to come in the apartment. Up here, the smell of bread permeated the rooms. She sank on the couch and he sat across from her.

"Are you that afraid of marriage?"

"No. I just don't want to marry someone you choose for me. I want to make the decision who I marry."

Why was this so difficult for him to understand? You would think it would be easy that she didn't want some rich, boring man who only married her for her money.

"But, Bella, you have wealth and your family name to think of. I don't want someone who would take advantage of my daughter."

Part of her wanted to laugh. It was a little late for that.

"And I don't want to be a commodity you are selling," she said to him.

He frowned. "I've never thought of my daughter as a commodity. I just want the best for you and felt that, as your father, I should make that decision for you."

"Why? Do you think I'm not capable of finding a good man?"

Maybe he was right. Obviously the man she'd fallen in love with had not been exactly perfect.

"Of course not, but there are predators out there who want to marry girls who have money. I don't want someone hurting you."

Too late, she thought, her heart breaking.

She thought for a moment as to how to make him understand. "Do you love, mother?"

"We've been together for almost twenty-five years."

He wasn't answering her question. In fact, he almost seemed uncomfortable.

"Who picked her out for you?" she asked.

He leaned back against the chair. "You have to understand. My family was not as prestigious as your mother's. We had new wealth but were not accepted because we were not of that social class. My father chose her for me. He made the deal with her father and paid his gambling debts."

Bella shook her head. "So your father chose who you were going to spend the rest of your life with. You can't tell me you love her and I know for a fact you keep a mistress on the side."

Her father's mouth dropped open and he sputtered. "Your mother is perfectly fine with it."

"Of course, she is because the two of you don't love one another. She was sold as a commodity just like you're trying to sell me," she said raising her voice. "And yes, it was noticeable to all the children. We knew there wasn't something right in our household. But we didn't know what. Now I know. And I am not going to let you choose my husband for me."

Her father's mouth meshed into a tight line across his face and his eyes looked tired. "Is there someone you want to marry?"

Stunned at the question, she didn't know how to answer. Yesterday, she would have answered yes, oh yes, but today she didn't have an answer for him. "I don't know. There was someone, but now…I just want to own my own business."

Her father threw up his hands. "I'm rich. You don't have to work. You have a trust fund that should easily take care of you."

He would never understand her love of the flour and the baking. Her love for the smell of the bread as it cooked.

"But I enjoy working. I enjoy baking and creating things with my hands. I don't just want to sit around doing nothing like I see my mother."

He laughed. "She is very good at that, isn't she?"

Her mother's life was nothing but one society function after another and that bored Bella to no end. She couldn't imagine what those women had to talk about all day besides what the latest gossip was and Bella didn't want to know.

"Yes, and I want to take care of myself."

"Yet your letter said you needed funds from your bank account."

"I did. I wanted to either buy the bakery or give Luca the money he needed for his vineyard. But now, now I don't know," she said. "I'm so disappointed."

Everything had fallen apart. She'd been going to present Luca with the necessary funds to buy the bakery she loved, but he didn't want to sell it to her. Oh no, he wanted to sell it to the meanest man in town, Tim Barton.

"Come home with me, baby girl. Come home and let me help you start a business in St. Louis."

She gazed at her father, seriously considering his offer. "You would help me? You wouldn't try to marry me off?"

He laughed. "I would help you. I would also introduce you to men I thought were appropriate, but I would not force you to marry them. As much as I hate to say it, I think you're right.

"I wish I had married a girl I met when I was your age. She was probably the love of my life, but I wasn't strong like my daughter. I let my father convince me to marry your mother. Who is a good woman, but she's not the love of my life."

Sadness overwhelmed Bella and she threw her arms around her father. "I'm so sorry, Father. But that explains so much. Thank you for telling me."

He sniffed. "Don't ever forget I love you. You're my daughter. And you are so much more like me than your mother."

She laughed, so happy and relieved she'd sent for her father. Yes, she loved her mother, but her father was the one who she related to. "I love you. Come down and see my bakery."

"I can't believe my daughter is a baker. You know your great-grandmother was an excellent cook."

She smiled. "Come see what I've created."

~

Franco hurried home to the vineyard where he saw his son, sitting on the wagon staring at the grapes. His horse galloped up to him and he slid to the ground. "What are you doing?"

"I'm thinking of burning the vineyard."

"No. This is your destiny. You must hold onto your dreams, but you can't destroy other people's dreams."

"I know and I let my greed take over. All I could think about was what I wanted."

Franco nodded, his son was learning a hard life lesson, but he had to tell him about Bella.

"You need to go to town and see Bella."

"She won't see me. I've already tried."

"Well, you need to try again. Her father is here. He wants her to return to St. Louis with him."

"St. Louis?" Luca said. "She told me she was from Boston."

"Well, he's from St. Louis and he's a very powerful man there. He wants her to come home with him. He wants her to marry some man."

Luca's eyes widened. "No, Papa. You have to help me. What can I do?"

"You go there and you get down on one knee and beg for forgiveness. You better pour your heart out to her or she will be gone."

Franco knew he was twisting the news just a little to his advantage, but he believed Luca and Bella were meant to be together. And he wanted their happiness.

Luca jumped off the wagon. "How did you propose to Mama?"

Franco laughed, feeling so much happiness inside. His son was in love and was going to ask this girl to marry him. His mama would be so happy if she were here.

"I took her flowers. I got down on one knee and told her she made me a happy man."

"But Mama was not angry with you."

"Yes, she was. I was a stupid pig-headed fool just like you. But she forgave me. If Bella is the right woman for you, she'll forgive you as well. Now go, son. Take my horse."

Luca climbed into the saddle, turned back to him, and smiled. "Thank you, Papa. Love you."

"Ciao," Franco said, watching as he clicked to the horse and headed to town.

Franco looked up at the sky. "Aw, Maria, I remember that day like yesterday. Miss you, il mio amore."

~

Bella didn't think this day could have any more highs or lows. Tim Barton was standing in front of her arguing about how he had paperwork to shut down the bakery.

"Let me see the paperwork," she said. "I'm not doing anything on your word."

His face turned red. "They're at my office. But by the order from the state, this bakery is to cease operations at once. You cannot own it."

"I don't own it," she said. She'd come down from visiting with her father to discover Tim harassing Callie and Diamond who just gave him a blank stare. "At least, not yet."

He sputtered. "You can't purchase the building because I already have a deal with Luca Ruffini. He's selling it to me."

"Good," she said. "But until my six weeks are up, you can't close me down. Now I'm sure you and he have cooked up some kind of deal to make certain I don't make a profit, but regardless, I get my six weeks. That doesn't end for two weeks. Now, either buy some bread or get out of my store."

"I'm not leaving," he said. "You can't throw me out."

"Fine. Stay if you want, but there is a barrel of flour that has your name on it if you don't leave."

His eyes widened. "You wouldn't."

"I probably wouldn't, but Diamond would. She's brasher than I am. She's already thrown out one man today and she wouldn't hesitate to make you the second."

Just then Diamond came from the back carrying not a barrel, but a sack of flour. "Sorry, but I couldn't lift the barrel."

"That will work just the same," Bella said.

She had put up with so much today, and she was at her limit, and this arrogant man who thought women were just objects to maneuver wanted her out of the bakery. If it had been anyone but him, she would have given up and gone home to St. Louis with her father, but this jackass made her realize what she was fighting for and he wasn't going to win.

"Last warning, leave or you will exit with flour all over you."

He drew up his body and started towards the door. "I will be contacting the sheriff and telling him about the threats you're making to me. You will be run out of town. My great-grandfather started this town, and as a member of the founding families, I don't deserve to be treated as such."

He whirled around and ran smack into the chest of her father. "Bella, is there a problem? I heard shouting clear up in the apartment."

"Yes, we have a rat we can't seem to get rid of."

"What's the problem," he said.

"I'm Tim Barton, a member of the founding family of this town, City Council member. Who are you, sir?"

"I'm George Francis, owner of the Francis Shipping Company out of St. Louis, soon to be governor of Missouri, and that's my daughter you're threatening."

Tim's eyes widened, and for the first time, Bella smiled. Her father was putting the family connections to good use.

"Now, you were going to talk to the law? And what was that I heard about shutting down my daughter's business?"

Tim licked his lips nervously. He glanced at Bella who stared at him. "All right, she can have two weeks, but then I insist she vacates the building as I will be purchasing it from the owner."

Her father's mouth pursed as he looked at Tim. "Hmm...last I heard, Bella was going to purchase the building. You know, she has the funds, and I think she's grown fond of your little town and the bakery."

His mouth dropped open. "But, but I need this space to build my hotel."

"Sorry, but it's occupied. Now, I think you should take home some bread to your wife. In fact, why don't you also take home some of those short-bread cookies? Those are delicious and your kids will be so happy you thought of them. And then...wait a minute." He paused. "Bella how much for everything you have in the cabinet this evening?"

"Oh, I think ten dollars would just about sum up the total for the bread and cookies and apple turnovers," she said with a laugh.

"Well, bag them up for Mr. Barton here. He has so generously agreed to buy you out this evening."

Callie and Diamond were laughing behind the counter as they wrapped everything up and put it into a paper sack.

Tim glared at her father, but opened his wallet and took out a ten dollar bill. He handed it to her and then grabbed the sack.

"Thank you, Mr. Barton," she called as he stomped out of the bakery.

The women all looked at each other and burst out laughing. She went to her father and hugged him. "Thank you."

"You're welcome."

Chapter Ten

Bella was in the back of the kitchen cleaning up after such a hectic day. She couldn't believe her father had made Tim Barton purchase the rest of her pastries, but felt like he deserved it after he'd treated them so badly.

The man was an arrogant ass whose wife was so sweet. Somehow they needed to convince that woman she should become a suffragette like them and learn how to stand up to that man.

Her father's confession that he'd been forced to marry her mother had made her sad. No wonder there was no love between them and that was exactly what she feared would happen to her if he found her a husband. She almost felt pity for her father and even for her mother.

Rolling out dough for tomorrow's bread, she heard the door open. What now?

She heard Callie say, "She doesn't want to see you."

"I don't care what she wants. She's going to see me."

Luca came storming to the back and Callie was running right behind him. "Give me a rolling pin. I'll straighten him out."

"No, let me take care of this. You stay out front."

"Are you sure?"

"Yes," Bella said as she picked up a small portion of the gooey dough in her bowl and threw it at him. It smacked him in the face and he stopped shocked. "What the hell?"

"That's for trying to ruin my dream."

She threw another piece of dough at him and it hit him in the chest. "That's for lying to me."

She threw another one and he caught it in his hand and threw it back, hitting her in the chest. "You also lied to me."

"I did not." She threw more dough at him, hitting him in the face.

He scraped the sticky substance off his face and threw it back to her hitting her on the neck.

"Oh, so you're from Boston. Your family is still there. And your last name is Sullivan?"

Oops. She'd forgotten all about telling him she was from Boston and faking her name. She was going to tell him the truth that afternoon they'd gone swimming, but instead they'd done other things.

"I was hiding."

"From what?" he asked his voice loud and urgent. "Tell me the truth."

"My father. He's here in town," she said, knowing he was upstairs in the apartment waiting for her.

"Well, it's still a lie," he said dodging another piece of dough. "We both made mistakes."

She aimed another dough ball at him and he advanced toward her. It hit him on the cheek. He growled and caught her arm just as she was about to unleash another barrage at him.

"You didn't want me to succeed."

He sighed. "You're wrong. I wanted you to succeed, but I wanted to sell the bakery. You are my il mio amore. I love you with all my heart. Yes, I started out trying to get your focus on me and not the bakery, but the very first kiss showed me what a fool I was to think I didn't want you.

"Then I was in turmoil because I knew if the bakery succeeded, my vineyard would not have the funds it needed. But now I don't care. The bakery is yours, just marry me and make me happy. My dream can wait."

Bella started to cry. It was all too much. The day had been fraught with heartache and forgiveness and redemption. She couldn't take anymore.

"I love you, Luca. I was so hurt that you wanted me to fail."

"I was stupid. I never want you to fail. I love your baking. I love you. I want us to marry and have bambinos. You are the other half of my soul. I need you."

She threw herself into his arms and he melded her mouth to his in a kiss that was nothing but pure flames. He moaned deeply in his throat and suddenly pulled back. "So will you marry me?"

"Yes," she said. "I love you so much."

"And I love you, mia Bella. But please don't throw dough at me anymore."

She giggled and reached up to swipe the flour from his face. "We seem to like getting flour on each other."

~

Two weeks later, the entire town was present for the double ring ceremony of Abigail and Jack, and Bella and Luca as they said their vows outside in the town square.

"I now present Mr. and Mrs. Ruffini," the preacher said. "And Mr. and Mrs. Turner."

Bella smiled at her husband and they turned to their family and friends and walked down the platform to the waiting reception. Luca squeezed her to him. "I'm the luckiest man alive."

She laughed. "You know I have a wedding present for you."

"And I have one for you as well," he said.

They walked past their friends and family until they reached the street. "Where are we going?"

"While we were getting married, I had some men changing the signs out at the bakery." They continued walking down the wooden sidewalk.

"Why?"

They stopped across the street from the bakery and she opened her eyes. "Oh my God. I love it."

The sign above the bakery now read "Bella's Bakery."

She threw her arms around Luca and hugged him.

"The bakery is yours, sweetheart. I completely relinquish all control and any money you earn from it. It's yours."

She leaned back and stared up into his dark eyes. "You needed the money for your vineyard."

"I also want my wife to be happy and your happiness is more important."

She smiled. "I also have a wedding present for you."

She grinned at him.

"Your father gave me the list of items you need for the vineyard, including the vines you wanted to order. They are on their way to you and I'm putting three thousand dollars in your new business account for the vineyard."

He stared at her, his eyes growing large. "Where did you get the money?"

She smiled. "My family is very wealthy. You married an heiress, and I want my husband who has sacrificed so much for me to also have his dreams realized. I want you to be even more successful than me."

Luca kissed her firmly, holding her body close to his. "You kept this a secret."

"Yes, my love. I wanted to surprise you. Now, you will have everything you need for the vineyard."

"Why didn't you buy the bakery from me when we first met?"

"I couldn't. I was hiding from my family and knew if I had any money sent to me, they would know where I was. After our fight, I went to the bank to try to get a loan, but they refused to lend to me because I'm a woman. But that will soon no longer be a problem."

He kissed her softly on the mouth. "Oh no...the suffragettes?"

Grinning, she gazed into his eyes and knew they were going to have a great life together. "Who else?"

He laughed. "I'm beginning to like these friends of yours. But I feel sorry for the Tim Bartons in this town. They have no clue about the hand they've been dealt."

~

Callie walked around the reception. Two of her friends married on the same day in the same service. When they had been in Boston, sitting in that jail, no one had planned on getting married. Now, just Callie, Diamond, and Georgia were single here in town.

Callie worried about Georgia. That girl was aching to find a man. And there were a lot of available men in town who would promise her the moon and the stars for a chance to marry a woman who would feed him and satisfy his sexual needs. But that wasn't what Callie wanted in life.

Her friends knew she had all the money she needed. Her mother had been one of the Randolph's and inherited more money than she could spend in a lifetime. And her father had invested his wife's money, tripling the amount. Unfortunately they died in a tragic carriage accident, leaving Callie alone.

Poor little rich girl, the papers had said. At seventeen, she'd inherited a million dollars, a passel of lowlife family members, and she'd awaken each morning to the yard in front of her house covered with men camping out wanting a chance to offer her marriage.

She'd been frightened, alone, and certain it was time to get out of town. So she'd gone from Los Angeles to Boston to attend school, hoping no one would recognize her. And for the most part, no one had. Then she'd become friends with Abigail and Bella. Together they'd marched for women's rights, gone to jail, and now were in Texas, still struggling for equality.

Gazing around at the wedding reception, she knew life had once again changed for them. But this time, she felt excitement. For suddenly, she knew what she wanted to do with her life. Like Abigail who'd learned she wanted to keep her inheritance, and Bella who loved baking, Callie realized what she could do to help bring change for women. She was just the woman to do it.

Glancing at Bella's father, she smiled. They had been talking and between the two of them they were going to change this little town.

"I handpicked your daughter for my son," Franco told Mr. Francis. "She won a baking contest and beat me. Then I got to know her and knew she was perfect for my Luca."

Bella's father smiled. "I like Luca and think he'll do great by my Bella. Her mother and I will be coming out often to visit."

"Very good. You know they will have beautiful bambinos. Your Bella's beauty and my son's strong will. Our families will be forever joined."

"And when Luca's vineyard starts producing good wine, then I will introduce his product to my friends."

Callie stepped up to the men. "Wait, just a minute. Let's let them have a honeymoon before you start giving them children."

Franco threw up his hands. "Maybe. But I can't wait to hold them in my arms. I just wish my Maria was here."

Shaking her head, Callie couldn't help but smile at the two proud fathers. "And Luca's vineyard will have an account at the new bank Mr. Francis and I plan on opening in town."

Franco's eyes widened. "What?"

George held his finger to his lips. "I'm going to help Miss Chesterfield open a bank. Bella was denied a loan by the local bank and since she has money, I don't want her to have to worry. So Callie and I will be opening a bank. She will be in charge and running it, but because of the atmosphere in this town, I will be on the board helping her."

"But how? Do you have the money to do that?"

Callie smiled. "I have a little money. This is my destiny."

Franco spoke rapidly in Italian. "Oh, you suffragettes are going to keep this town jumping." He laughed. "And I get to see it all. You need a husband. Too bad my youngest boy is too young."

"No, I don't need a husband. But I may need a guard."

Look for Callie's story coming soon!

Thank you for reading!

Dear Reader,

Thank you for taking the time to read *Bella*. If you enjoyed it, please consider telling your friends or posting a few words on your favorite vendor's website. Whether or not you loved the book or hated, it – I'd enjoy your feedback.

If you enjoy western historical authors, please join the Pioneer Hearts group on Facebook. This is a fabulous group of readers and authors who enjoy westerns.

Sign up for my newsletter at sylviamcdaniel.com if you'd like to learn about my new releases as soon as possible.

Reading one of my books is like spending time with me, and I just want to say thank you from the bottom of my heart.

Yours in Drama, Divas, Bad Boys, and Romance!

Sincerely,
Sylvia McDaniel

Books by Sylvia McDaniel

Contemporary Romance

Standalones
The Reluctant Santa
My Sister's Boyfriend
The Wanted Bride
The Relationship Coach
Her Christmas Lie
Secrets, Lies, and Online Dating
Paying for the Past
Cupid's Revenge

Anthologies
Kisses, Laughter & Love
Christmas with you

Collaborative Series

Magic, New Mexico
Touch of Decadence

Western Historicals

Standalones
A Hero's Heart
A Scarlet Bride
Second Chance Cowboy

The Cuvier Women
Wronged
Betrayed
Beguiled

Lipstick and Lead
Desperate
Deadly
Dangerous
Daring
Determined
Deceived

Scandalous Suffragettes
Abigail
Bella
Callie
Faith

The Burnett Brides
The Rancher Takes a Bride
The Outlaw Takes a Bride
The Marshal Takes a Bride
The Christmas Bride

Anthologies
Wild Western Women
Courting the West
Wild Western Women Ride Again

Collaborative Series

The Surprise Brides
Ethan

American Mail Order Brides
Katie

About the Author

Sylvia McDaniel is a best-selling, award-winning author of historical romance and contemporary romance novels. Known for her sweet, funny, family-oriented romances, Sylvia is the author of The Burnett Brides, a western historical western series, The Cuvier Widows, a Louisiana historical series, and several short contemporary romances.

She is the former President of the Dallas Area Romance Authors, a member of the Romance Writers of America®, and a member of Novelists Inc. Her novel, A Hero's Heart, was a 1996 Golden Heart Finalist. Several other books have placed or won in the San Antonio Romance Authors Contest and the LERA Contest, and she was a Golden Network Finalist.

Married for nearly twenty years to her best friend, they have two dachshunds that are beyond spoiled and a good-looking, grown son who thinks there's no place like home. She loves gardening, shopping, knitting, and football (Cowboys and Bronco's fan), but not necessarily in that order.

Look for her the first Tuesday of every month at the Plotting Princesses blogspot, and be sure to sign up for her newsletter to learn about new releases and contests. Every month a new subscriber is entered into a drawing for a free book!

She can be found online at: www.sylviamcdaniel.com or on Facebook. You can write to Sylvia at P.O. Box 2542, Coppell, TX 75019.

Looking for a new book to read?

<u>Check out Abigail</u>

Women Wanted – Feisty, Head-Strong Women Need Not Apply

In New Hope, Texas women like children, are to be seen and not heard. Their only job in life is to marry, procreate, and be a loyal, obedient wife. Thus the shortage of available women. Until, Abigail Vanderhooten is unexpectedly called home, her head filled with ideas of changing the world where a woman can own a business and have a bank account. This little rebel is determined to bring the town's laws into the nineteenth century, even if it means sacrificing her reputation.

Jack Turner likes being the mayor in a small, quiet western town where the biggest rabble rousers are cowboys on Saturday night. Everything is about to change when Abigail Vanderhooten, a tiny sprite of a woman returns to town, ready to take on the local laws. While trying to keep the town from splitting apart, he's surprised how her strong spirit captivates him. And he's shocked when she manages to worm her way into his bachelor heart, with her controversial ideas of women earning a living the same as a man.

With a woman's revolution brewing, will Jack be forced to run her out of town, before he has a chance to convey how she's changed him? Or will Abigail give up on New Hope, Texas and return to Boston?

Can love blossom and change a woman and a man with different ideals?

Sneak Peek into Abigail: Scandalous Suffragette!

Abigail Vanderhooten wasn't a thief, a prostitute, a murderer, or a cheat. But here she sat with all of her friends in the Boston city jail. What was their crime? Being a woman!

Women had so few rights. No bank accounts, no land, and no vote. And owning a business was frowned upon in many cities and outlawed in others. Their sole purpose in life was to become a wife and mother. Marry, procreate, and make their husband look good. Sit down, shut-up, and look pretty.

Well, Abigail and her friends wanted more. Much more and after attending Matilda Joslyn Gage's speech at the National Women's Suffrage Association's convention, they'd made a commitment to change the world.

Except, they'd hit a small snag. The Boston city police took exception to them blocking the entrance to one of the local banks. And now here they were waiting in jail.

"Abigail, I want to draw attention to a woman's plight, but I'm not certain my daddy is going to keep paying for me to attend Boston University if I keep getting thrown in jail. If my mother finds out, she's going to take a switch to my hide," Callie said, shifting on the hard wooden floor.

The cell held nothing more than one cot, a slop jar, and the eight of them. They'd been in here since yesterday afternoon, and they were exhausted, hungry, and so ready to go back to their dorms.

"Callie, we must all make sacrifices to bring about a difference."

Faith leaned back against the wall and crossed her arms over her chest. "Maybe we're going about this wrong. Maybe we should start our own town."

"Which one of us is going to construct the buildings?" Bella asked.

Abigail sighed and thought about Faith's idea. Maybe it would be simpler to just start fresh somewhere and make up their own laws. Their chances of getting what they needed would be a lot easier. "There are going to be things we don't have the strength to do, but we hire men for what we need that we can't provide. Being an independent woman doesn't mean we don't need men. We just want more control over our own destiny."

"Good, because I kind of like men," Diamond said with a giggle, pushing back her red hair. The most beautiful of them all, she said her stage actress mother had named her daughter after her favorite jewel her most recent suitor had given her.

"Oh dear," Emma said, shaking her head. "You've lost the spirit of the movement. We're learning to be independent from men and playing kissy face with them does not help the cause."

Abigail sat back and looked at each of her friends. "Tell me what you would do if we did build our own town? And what would bring families and men to this town?"

"I'd be a baker," Bella said. "You know how much I love to bake."

"I think I gained ten pounds off that last batch of crumpets you made. Gosh, those were good. But that's a woman's job," Georgia said. "I'm hungry."

Abigail nodded her head, agreeing with her friend. But they had to have bigger ambitions.

"I don't know. I just don't want to do what my mother has done all her life. Do you know what it's like for a woman who has nine kids in twelve years?" Haley said softly.

An only child, Abigail would have liked to have had more brothers and sisters. It was just her and her father, since her mother died when she was twelve. And then her father, at her mother's insistence, had sent her back East for her education on how to be a proper young woman.

Wouldn't he be shocked to learn she was in jail for protesting the banks' regulations regarding women?

"Me, I'd like to be a doctor. I'm going to help women by studying how to keep from getting pregnant. Having a baby every two to three years kills a lot of women," Emma replied.

Of all the girls, besides Abigail, in this march to liberate women, Emma was the smartest, and she would graduate from the university at the end of the month. Someday, she would be an excellent healer, and already, she was working with the national organization, talking to women about how not to conceive a baby every nine months.

Quiet, shy Callie lifted her head and glanced at each of them. "I want to open a bank. Give women bank accounts and loan them money. I would advance each of you whatever it was you needed to start your business."

Diamond, the most flamboyant one of the group, laughed. "I just want to have fun. If I can have fun and run a business, I will. If not, then I'm going to find a way. I'm tired of all this seriousness. Yes, I want to help women, but sitting here inside a jail cell is not my idea of a good time."

Abigail's mother would have considered Diamond to be an improper young woman. But Abigail knew that beneath all the flash and flamboyant speech was a scared girl afraid of returning to her mother.

"Maybe you need to open a saloon," Faith said, and they knew she was being facetious.

"Maybe I will. I could sing and maybe even dance," Diamond said. "I just don't want to go back to my family and watch my mother entertain her newest gentleman friend."

father, at her mother's insistence, had sent her back East for her education on how to be a proper young woman.

Wouldn't he be shocked to learn she was in jail for protesting the banks' regulations regarding women?

"Me, I'd like to be a doctor. I'm going to help women by studying how to keep from getting pregnant. Having a baby every two to three years kills a lot of women," Emma replied.

Of all the girls, besides Abigail, in this march to liberate women, Emma was the smartest, and she would graduate from the university at the end of the month. Someday, she would be an excellent healer, and already, she was working with the national organization, talking to women about how not to conceive a baby every nine months.

Quiet, shy Callie lifted her head and glanced at each of them. "I want to open a bank. Give women bank accounts and loan them money. I would advance each of you whatever it was you needed to start your business."

Diamond, the most flamboyant one of the group, laughed. "I just want to have fun. If I can have fun and run a business, I will. If not, then I'm going to find a way. I'm tired of all this seriousness. Yes, I want to help women, but sitting here inside a jail cell is not my idea of a good time."

Abigail's mother would have considered Diamond to be an improper young woman. But Abigail knew that beneath all the flash and flamboyant speech was a scared girl afraid of returning to her mother.

"Maybe you need to open a saloon," Faith said, and they knew she was being facetious.

"Maybe I will. I could sing and maybe even dance," Diamond said. "I just don't want to go back to my family and watch my mother entertain her newest gentleman friend."

The sound of a door opening made Abigail glance up from the floor, where they were all sitting. She watched as a policeman approached the cell.

"Ladies, I'm going to let you go with a warning. Any other demonstrations will result in fines. Are we clear?"

Clear as mud was the response Abigail wanted to declare, but she was ready to get out of this cell. Sitting on a wooden floor was not her idea of luxury.

"Mrs. Minor is vouching for you, and I've agreed to let you go in her custody. No more demonstrations."

"I thought we lived in America, the land of the free," Emma said.

The policeman frowned. "These are my terms. You can accept them or stay in jail, and I'll telegraph each one of your families. Your choice."

"Abigail, I can't have my papa finding out we went to jail," Bella said.

Bella's father was searching for a suitable match for her—a man who would increase the family's financial empire. Abigail thought he should just hang a price tag around his daughter's neck. The result would be the same.

These ladies were all fighting not only for their independence, but the right to choose and marry a man they were in love with. Not a man who would elevate their financial status in the world.

"I want to go back to our dorm," Faith said quietly. "I'm tired."

"Let's not concede defeat. Let's stay and fight," Diamond replied.

Just then, Mrs. Minor stepped into the jail area. "Girls, it's time to give up." She waved an envelope. "Abigail, I have a telegram for you from home."

"Ladies, before I open this door, I need you to tell me you understand. No more protests or I will fine you so badly you'll have to contact your families to get out of jail."

"Oh, all right," Abigail said, a trickle of worry scurrying along her spine like a rat deserting a sinking ship. "I need to read that message."

"Now, ladies, no more trouble. Boston has had enough of you." The officer opened the jail door with a clang.

Abigail rushed to Mrs. Minor, and she handed over the telegram.

COME HOME. YOUR FATHER IS ILL.

A pang zipped through Abigail's body, and her chest clenched with pain. He must be bad if they'd sent for her. She knew what she had to do.

"Ladies, my father is ill. I'm catching the next train to Fort Worth."

www.ingramcontent.com/pod-product-compliance
Lightning Source LLC
Chambersburg PA
CBHW071829190726
48292CB00005B/1692